Edward Robeson Taylor

Moods and Other Verses

Edward Robeson Taylor

Moods and Other Verses

ISBN/EAN: 9783743441750

Manufactured in Europe, USA, Canada, Australia, Japa

Cover: Foto ©Andreas Hilbeck / pixelio.de

Manufactured and distributed by brebook publishing software (www.brebook.com)

Edward Robeson Taylor

Moods and Other Verses

MOODS
AND OTHER VERSES

BY

EDWARD ROBESON TAYLOR

" Not for arrogant pride
Nor over boldness fail they who have striven
To tell what they have heard, with voice too weak
For such high message. More it is than ease,
Palace and pomp, honours and luxuries,
To have seen white Presences upon the hill
To have heard the voices of the Eternal Gods."

Epic of Hades.—Sir LEWIS MORRIS.

"The least of us is not too weak
To leave the world with something done."

Palinode.—EDMUND GOSSE.

D. P. ELDER & MORGAN SHEPARD
SAN FRANCISCO
1899

TO MY WIFE

AGNES STANFORD TAYLOR

HADST THOU NOT SERVED MY WAYWARD MOOD,
NOR LET MY LEISURE HAVE ITS WAY,
'TIS TRUTH TO SAY THIS LITTLE BROOD
OF VERSE WOULD NOT HAVE SEEN THE DAY;
EXCEPT THE CRUDE, IMPERFECT RHYMES
I COUPLED IN THE FAR-OFF TIMES,
WHEN DIVINATION COULD NOT SEE
WHAT THY FOND HEART SHOULD BRING TO ME;
AND IF THE MUSES NOW ENTWINE
THE SLENDEREST THREAD ROUND BROW OF MINE,
ONE HALF THE GLORY SHALL BE THINE.

TABLE OF CONTENTS

x

Moods

" Blest is the man who with the sound of song
  Can charm away the heartache, and forget
The frost of penury and stings of wrong,
  And drown the fatal whisper of regret!
        Darker are the abodes
          Of Kings, tho' his be poor,
        While Fancies, like the Gods,
          Pass thro' his door."
    The Skylark and the Poet.—FREDERICK TENNYSON.

" In common things that round us lie
  Some random truths he can impart,—
The harvest of a quiet eye
  That broods and sleeps on his own heart."
              A Poet's Epitaph.—WORDSWORTH.

MY MUSE

If that my Muse can never hope to soar
  Above the summits where unwasting snows
  Are fellows of the stars;—if that she knows
  No swelling note of forest, sea, or shore;—
If e'en no streamlet of melodious lore
  The tiniest craft of hers divinely shows;—
  Or not for her the lightest breeze that blows
  In voiceful harmony Parnassus o'er;—
Yet her dear self I could not think to chide,
  Nor deem her less than some anointed saint
  Who guards my soul: sufficient unto me
If in my deepest being she abide,
  To hold my wandering thoughts in sweet constraint,
  And all that's noblest give me sight to see.

DREAM

It may be that in some auspicious hour,
    When all life's currents run serenely free,
    A voice will come from Dreamland unto me
    Upborne on music of celestial power.
Then in the garden of my heart some flower
    May burst to bloom in sudden ecstasy,
    And with delightful, deathless fragrancy
    Add mite of glory to the Poet's dower.
O soul, thou feedest on the husks of hope,
    And starvest while the things within thy scope
    Lie all before thee in their bounty spread.
And yet, ah, let me for at least to-day
    Enjoy the vision ere it melts away,
    To be with other dreams forever fled.

MY LADY SLEEPS

TO A. S. T.

My lady sleeps, and sleeps in sweetest peace;
   No stain of tear is on her restful face,
   While placid smiles do there each other chase,
   To give assurance of her pain's release.
Her radiant head, that doth the pillow crease
   In such serene repose, I fain would kiss
   Till heart and soul were emptied of all bliss,
   And love itself gave thankfulness surcease.
O Sleep, thou top of blessings! What to thee
   Does grief-struck, pain-tormented man not owe,
   Or how, without thee, from his miseries flee?
And now that thou my lady's couch dost know,
   From torture's agony to set her free,
   Thou beamest on me with divinest glow.

TO SLEEP

Thou angel Sleep, when I recall to mind
  The sons of Genius, who on soaring wing
  Have sung of thee the choicest they could sing,
  In jeweled phrases goldenly enshrined
In love perennial of humankind,
  I scarce durst try to body forth the note
  That swells within my unmelodious throat,
  Craving some fitting utterance to find;
But when thou cam'st on yesternight to me,
  And stroked so tenderly my feverous head,
  That thought and sense to sweet oblivion's sea
From every grief and irritation fled,
  My grateful heart became so full of thee,
  That, scoff who may, my Muse and thou must wed.

REVERIE

What realm is thine, thou gentle ruler, Sleep!
   All life obeys thee, while earth's countless graves
   But point to where thy ageless banner waves,
   And where thou dost unbroken vigil keep.
Innumerous messengers are thine, who leap
   To do thy bidding—noiseless, nimble knaves,
   Who bring from out thy many-chambered caves
   Sweet dreams wherein the troubled brain to steep.
And from thy choicest chamber steals thy child
   Poetic souls do know as Reverie;
   'Tis she whose fingers set the spirit free,
So that from every fleshly hindrance isled,
   It may with Fancy roam the woodland wild,
   Or sail upon Imagination's sea.

HOME

TO A. S. T. AND P. C. L.

Of earthly things thou greatest blessing—Home!
Safe refuge where the overburdened soul
Lays down its weary weight of toil and care,
To gain refreshment in the arms of rest.
In deep dreams there the frets of life are hushed,
Its turmoils and its woes, while the stopped ears
Hear nought of clamor's unrelenting noise
That roars tumultuous in the world without.
And there the mistress of the blest abode
In sweetest tyranny serenely sways
Her silver sceptre over all the house,
Until each feverous, discordant pulse,
Ruled by the music of her bounteous love,
Beats to the measure of harmonious peace.

PRAYER

Thou Power divine man feels so well
   Yet in thy fullness never knows,
That in the humblest weed doth dwell,
   As in the queenliest rose that blows,
And in the tides of all the seas,
   And in the heart of man and beast;
That soundest all the harmonies
   From nature's greatest to her least;

Mayhap no merely human prayer
   Addressed to thee can aught avail;
Mayhap thy forces have no care
   For joyful song or woeful wail;—
But when with weariness we faint,
   When burdens crush, or griefs dismay,
When faiths have lost their old restraint,
   We fall upon our knees to pray.

And wherefore should we not, if thou
   Art what we fain believe thou art—
If thou thy presence dost avow

In all the beatings of our heart?
Call then, O Soul, thine angels blest;
  Drive out the host of bestial sin;
Plant conquering courage in the breast,
  And let the spirit's glory in.

CONSOLATION

The world is hard, and selfishness supreme;
The love of man for man is all a dream,
And e'en Religion but a worn-out theme . . .
    Ofttimes it seemeth so.
Still, souls there are who do themselves forget;
Man strives and bleeds for man; and even as yet
Religion soothes us in our toil and fret . . .
    Ofttimes 'tis surely so.

THE POET

He crushed his heart for wine of song
  With which the soul of man to glad;
But who of all the careless throng
  Could dream how mad he was—how mad!

10

PROOF OF GOD

Dost ask for *proof* of God ?—Thou mayst as well
  Ask of the daisy, as it meekly blows,
  Whence cometh it, or how, or why it grows;
  Or pray the world-compelling genius tell
The secret cunning of his magic spell;—
  But when their hearts lie close against thine own
  Until their pulse-beats thrill thee to the bone,
  Doubt's demons perish in their self-made hell.
The wings of Reason beat themselves in vain
  Against the ether of a soundless air,
  To fold at last in logic's dull despair.
Divinely ordered is this fruitless lore:
  For were God *proved,* all mystery would be plain,
  And man himself, as man, could be no more.

THOUGHTS

A dream came o'er me, and I thought
   A hundred ships, blown from the East,
To me had rarest cargoes brought,
   With which to make a wondrous feast.

But as the ships at anchor lay,
   A storm-wind blew from out the West,
And when I looked, at break of day,
   No ships were seen, no bidden guest.

———————

We cannot all be wisely great,
   Much less be greatly wise;
To few alone is't given by fate
   To read the mysteries,
And in the mass of rubbish find
The food that nourishes mankind—
   But none there is who cannot move
   The world a little with his love.

The child holds out its loving hand
For gifts supplied from fairyland;
Life lies for it in smiles and tears,
Unvexed by doubt, unharmed by fears.

Youth sees beyond the fairyland,
And having life's horizon scanned,
It swells with self-conceit to know
That all is plain from high to low.

In manhood knowledge brings her lore,
To gender doubts still more and more,
Until at last it dares to know
That all is dark and will be so.

But through the dark the sage shall see
The stars that light the life to be,
Assured he shall forever grow,
But never can completely know.

———————

The deepest poem is the one we feel,
And not the one that language can reveal;
Oh, times there are when music stirs the soul
Beyond mere words to measure or control,

Thoughts And myriad thoughts flit ghostlike through the brain
That all the tongues of earth could never chain.
Let artist paint with ne'er so deep a speech,
Great worlds there are he cannot hope to reach.

———

One doubts, one fears, one calls on circumstance,
And one is blown by every wind of chance;
While yet another looks into his soul,
And sails serenely to his destined goal.

———

Like him who, drawn by glorious heights beyond,
Is forced to cross the intervening flood
By dangerous step from slippery stone to stone,
So we, in this tumultuous life, but step
In trembling from one trouble to another,
While Error waits with her remorseless train
In hope to whelm us in the raging wave.

NOW

Oh, do not wait until in earth I lie
Before thou givest me my rightful meed;
Oh, do not now in coldness pass me by,
And then cry praises which I cannot heed.
If I have helped thee on thy weary way,
Or lightened in the least thy burden's weight,
Haste with love's tokens ere another day
Shall pierce thee with the fatal words, "Too late."
The present moment is thy time to live:
The Past is gone, the Future may not be;
If thou hast treasure of thy heart to give
To hungry souls, bestow it speedily;—

    For sweet Love's sake, let not to-morrow's sun
    Tempt thee to wait before thou see it done.

ATTAINMENT

We sigh for things we scarce may hope to gain,
  And which, if all our own, would give no peace;
  We vainly toil and struggle to release
  To knowledge nature's secrets; we complain
That 'tis not given us to break some chain,
  To scale some peak, to fetch some golden fleece,
  To do some mighty deed whose light shall cease
  Only when moons no longer wax and wane.
'Tis thus we make a mockery of life,
  And miss the blessing at our very hand:
  For Faith and Love, with glory as of sun,
Illume the path to Peace through every strife;
  No work is futile that is nobly planned;
  No deed is little if but greatly done.

SUFFICIENCY

Let vulgar Malice work its venomed will
   Against the heart that would have given its blood
   To shield the thing which strikes it; let the brood
   Of Envy swarm like bees a-hiving, and distil
Poisons more sure than those of Borgian skill;
   Let Friendship wither, and a common good
   No more be nourished by her nectared food;
   And even dear Love insanely stab and kill.
Let all this be, with ills as yet unguessed;
   And still, thou shalt as ocean wind be free,
   If bravely thou dost seek thy strength and rest
Within thyself, bending compliant knee
   To Conscience only, and in peace possessed
   Of that all-crowning grace—Humility.

CONCENTRATION

TO L. C. L.

Mark how the florist's cunning hand compels
 That weed unique, the strange chrysanthemum,
 To crown one lonely stalk whose blossomed sum
 To giant size and gorgeous beauty swells—
The forces pulsing in its myriad cells
 Concentring all their magic and their power
 To build the structure of a single flower,
 Wherein the plant its dazzling triumph tells.
So shouldst thou have the will, O struggling soul,
 To hold thy thoughts and actions to the pole
 Of one imperious, exclusive aim;
Then may *thy* stalk a wondrous blossom bear,
 Which shall for thee achievement's glory wear,
 And be to others as a sign of flame.

"Long have I sued, and still have sued in vain;—
My one and only love, why holdst me off
With laughing banter and with bitter scoff?
Wilt never ease my heart's unceasing pain?"
"If thou'lt be brave," said she, "thy sorrow's rain
Shall breed a harvest; look! seest thou yon peak
That lifts at dizzy height its snowy beak?
Bear me to that, and thou my heart shalt drain."
Upon his back he took the tempting maid,
And upward went; up and still up he strode,
The distant, glittering peak his constant guide;
Still up, o'er Alp on Alp, he strained, nor stayed
Till to the pinnacle he bore his load—
Then like an idiot laughed . . . and gasping . . .
    died.

THE OLD, OLD DAYS

TO L. M. L. AND J. A. Q.

O golden-hearted, richly-hallowed days
  That loom through deepening mists on memory's
    shore,
  When boyhood fed from joy's unmeasured store
  As hope sang loud her sweetest roundelays!
How romped we in the wood's far-opening ways
  When irksome studies for the time were o'er;
  How plied we games in their abounding lore,
  How felt as gods when victory led to praise!
The Master's strenuous voice ceased long ago,
  While few of all that throng on earth can be,
  And these are burdened with the weight of years;
Yet on that fruitful spot still others glow
  With youthful fire and sport the same as we,
  Undreamt the future's agonies and tears.

SOLITUDE

Thy aid I supplicate, O Solitude,
  For one sore wounded in the unending strife
  That makes such burden of our daily life;
  Let me with thy repose be deep imbrued;
On thy smooth stream bear off each feverous mood,
  And float my spirit to the Isles of Calm
  Where grows luxuriant thy healing balm,
  And where mad clamor never may intrude.
Where thou wilt take me it doth matter not,
  For where thou art my spirit's peace will be;
  The mind, fresh-winged, will rise to nobler thought,
And radiant sprites from Dreamland visit me,
  As from my covert, with fresh beauties fraught
  Looms Life's vast, varicolored, pulsing sea.

POETIC ART

The cities vanish; one by one
The glories go that glories won;
At Time's continuous, fateful call
The palaces and temples fall;
While heroes do their deeds and then
Sink down to earth as other men.
Yet, let the Poet's mind and heart
But touch them with the wand of Art,
And lo! they rise and shine once more
In greater splendor than before.

LIFE AND DEATH

Life is not all in all,
  Nor yet is Death;
But from the Vast they call,
  And each one saith:
I am the one in whom thy being lies;
Accept thy fate, nor fear me when I rise.

ADVERSITY

O friend, when glad Fortuna comes to thee
   With hands that offer more than liberal spoils,
   Beware, lest slyly hid a serpent coils,
   Thy soul to poison with Prosperity.
Thou never canst seraphic visions see
   As noble recompense for strenuous toils,
   Unless within thy deepest being boils
   Some tear-fed fountain of Adversity.
The steel that Florence drove in Dante's heart
   He fashioned to a lyre whereon with ease
   He deathless rose above the hells of hate ;
And when life-wearied Milton sat apart,
   Lonely and blind, he swept those organ keys
   Whose tones from age to age reverberate.

REFUGE

TO PROFESSOR ALBIN PUTZKER

The winds of grief were driving him
  Upon the rocks despair had reared,
When in the distance faintly dim
  The Star of Poesy appeared;
And as toward her his face he turned
  With hope and courage in his breast,
She then with great refulgence burned,
  To light him to the port of Rest.

QUESTION

Outside, the rain is dreary,
Inside, my heart is weary;
Outside, the winds are sighing,
Inside, my hopes are dying;
O Earth, where is thy beauty?
O Soul, where is thy duty?

24

TO THE SONNET

Bound in the fetters of thy narrow frame
  What souls have conquered song!—Here Dante's
    woe,
  As Petrarch's, swells to joy; here Angelo
  Greatens the glory of his mighty name;
'Tis here that Shakespeare bares his breast to blame,
  And here that Milton stoops, great strains to blow;
  Here Wordsworth's notes with rapturing music flow,
  While Keats divinely glows with quenchless flame.
Yea, all the rhymsters of our modern day
  Crowd round thy shrine, and beg thee to enring
  Their brows with leaves of thy immortal bay;
Such crown is not for me, but prithee fling
  Thy spell upon me, so at least I may
  Yet dream of beauties I can never sing.

ENDEAVOR

I

" I discern
Vain aspiration,—unresultive work,"
—*Mrs. Browning's " Prometheus Bound " of Æschylus.*

Still am I tossed upon a troubled sea,

   Puzzled and doubting how to make my way;

   Resultless day follows resultless day,

   And even my dreams no solace bring to me.

At Duty's call, unheeding other plea,

   Have I pushed forward, scornful of delay,

   Ne'er yielding sense to indolence's sway,

   Nor grieving over what might never be.

And now, the years seem shorter as they run,

   Nor dares my life to hope for many more,

   Or should they come, that they will truly bless.

The best that lay within me has been done;

   And as an end all vainly I deplore

   Endeavor's dreary waste of fruitlessness.

II

Thou wavering soul, what note is this to sound?   *Endeavor*

   Dost prate of Duty, yet art satisfied

   With what thou hast in scarce half-struggle tried?

   Dost beat thy wings against thy self-made bound,

Forgetful that in Life's unresting round

   All marvellously wondrous things abide

   For him who seeks and will not be denied?

   And that the humblest may not go uncrowned?

O blinded one, unhood thy spirit's eyes,

   So they may truly see the world without,

   And that still other world which stirs within;

Then canst thou soar above thy miseries

   To heights undarkened by the clouds of Doubt,

   And where to Victory thou mayst be kin.

SONG ITS OWN REWARD

TO JOHN MUIR

Song is its own reward, so said to me
  My clear-eyed, toiling friend whose jewelled prose
  With joy of being sings as on it flows,
  Bearing the thoughts that teach us to be free;
Thou shouldst not hush one note of Poesy
  That from Parnassian heights rejoicing blows,
  Though none of all the world its music knows,
  Or knowing cares for, saving only thee.
O friend, thou nursling of the mountain's breast,
  True brother of the glacier and the pine,
  'Tis meet *thy* voice this lesson has impressed;
For do not all these noble kin of thine
  Ring out forevermore their strains divine
  Though not one soul may hearken to be blest!

THE DIVINE HARMONY

TO MRS. L. C. LANE

A single soul—what microscopic mite
   When measured '*gainst* the universe of things!
   A voice that for a moment sobs and sings,
   And then seems lost in silence of the night.
But yet how great the meanest, merest sprite
   When measured *in* the universe of things!
   For there 'tis one with earth's supremest kings,
   And bathes in unextinguishable light.
It must be that the note of every soul
   Is needed in the harmonies that roll
   And throb eternally with power divine;
And I, dear friend, when stars were fair to see,
   Have drank the summit's deep delights with thee,
   As shone refulgent the assuring sign.

29

TO A MARBLE STATUETTE OF
BEATRICE

When youthful Dante's roving, marvellous eyes
   Upon the universe began to ope
   As if with presage of their future scope,
   They saw thy great original arise ;
And then he thrilled as one divinely wise,
   For well he knew the star of faith and hope
   That should lead on his travailing soul to cope
   With all the hells beneath storm-clouded skies.
And now in marble spotless as her name
   Thou dost compel such tribute to her fame
   As if her own deep gaze upon us beamed ;
For thine the art wherein we newly see
   Some hint of that which Dante greatly dreamed
   Of woman's loveliness and purity.

DAWN

TO JAMES ADDISON QUARLES

Now radiant Dawn unlocks her roseate doors,
  Whence all her featly-footed, swarming band
  Streams swift along the sleep-encompassed land,
  And in the skies on fiery pinion soars.
The pauseless glory sweeps by moaning shores
  Where Storm's poor victims strew the shuddering
      strand,
  While from the heights where trees rejoicing stand
  It through my lady's window softly pours.
And as the fulgent beams grow still more bright,
  Man flees the darker deeds of tempting Night
  And meets with fresh resolve the new-born Day.
My dear old friend, when comes to us anon
  That earthly Night no power can roll away,
  May we together greet a newer Dawn.

31

THE UNFINISHED PORTRAIT

TO W. K. AND E. M.

"I cannot strike the color for this eye,
  Nor bend the arch above it;—ah, to-day
  My brush's cunning, do the best I may,
  In very mockery fain would pass me by."
Thus spake the Master as he stood anigh
  His easel, where a young man's portrait lay
  So near to perfectness it seemed to say,
  Give me not up ere once again you try.
Then with a fury such as genius knows,
  He spread his pigments all that portrait o'er
  Until a landscape shone divinely there;
And in the glories of its great repose
  Imagination feels, as ne'er before,
  Some hidden spirit breathe through all the air.

LOVE'S FEARS

Thou dost not love me—that I see;
    So let us part,
Although I feel it means to me
    A breaking heart.

But better thus than have thee near
    From day to day,
And freeze with oft-recurring fear
    That love's away.

One chilling kiss, and all is o'er
    Between us twain,
And then, and then, perchance no more
    To meet again;

No more to have thy presence fill
    My leisure hours;
No more to know that earth has still
    For me some flowers.

No more means much;—that thou and I
    Life's wine could drink
From different cups and peace not die,
    'Twere vain to think.

'Tis past;—I feel, when drawing nigh
  The fateful edge,
Affection come with stronger tie
  And newer pledge.

We cannot part—the love of years
  Shall not be slain
By all the misbegotten fears
  That e'er caused pain.

Then let the darkness leave thine eye,
  And on thy breast
My all forgiven, foolish cry
  Be hushed to rest.

SONG

I dare be sworn thou lov'st me; but thy word
Is so at odds with what thou dost accord,
That torn with doubt I oft do sadly fain
To never look upon thy face again.

But when once more thy beauty fills mine eye,
Thou art to me all things beneath the sky,
And then, despite all doubt, I fondly fain
To never lose thee from my sight again.

34

SONG

Always be the same, sweetheart,
Or we must forever part;
Smiles to-day and frowns to-morrow
Can but bring us anxious sorrow;
Be the same as now thou art,
And we shall not, cannot, part.

Do I doubt thee?—never! never!—
Love shall hold us fast forever;
Folded in thine eager arms,
Life for me can have no harms;
Pillowed on thy fragrant breast,
Come what may I must be blest.

MY SUMMER

Winter once more comes on apace
  With chilling wind and lowering sky,
But summer still makes glad thy face,
  And in its warmth I restful lie.

DELIVERANCE

IN MEMORY OF J. T. H.

Thus spake my friend:—What bliss can fill the breast
   When drawn from deepest wells of dark despair,
   I knew not till I ventured forth to fare
   On ocean's paths by tempest's wrath possessed:
Throughout the night in fearsome, sick unrest,
   We felt our helpless ship reel blindly where
   Storm's unexhausted legions filled the air
   And rode with fury on each billow's crest.
But when the last dim ray of hope seemed gone,
   The winds drew off, and long-awaited dawn
   With beauty's topmost glory lit the sea;
And as the sun above the horizon shone,
   Beyond the waves with many a rainbow sown
   I saw my child once more upon my knee.

WORK

To age-worn palace veiled with vine and tree
   I listless came one summer afternoon,
   A self-invited guest who craved the boon
   Of peaceful idlesse in that privacy.
And then, as swung the portal back for me,
   I saw some inmates lounge as half in swoon,
   While others gaped and yawned, tried trivial tune,
   Turned a few leaves, then wandered aimlessly.
And when Ennui, the jewelled queen of these,
   Uprising from her bed of poppied ease,
   Drawled greeting such as indolence could spare,
I fled aghast the humblest tool to seize,
   And as its strokes with music filled the air
   Peace spread her wings in holy blessing there.

The demon Sawmill said, I lack for food
    Wherewith to cram this craving maw of mine,
    That spite of nature and of law divine
    Would gorge on all that's grandest in the wood.
Then they who madly serve the monster's good,
    Mid jocund laughter, slew a giant pine,
    As bright-eyed, cheery morn with flaming sign
    Awoke to life the slumbering solitude.
For immemorial years this fallen one
    Had been so loved by earth and air and sun,
    It seemed with beauty for the ages clad;
And as its massive trunk and members lie
    Dissevered and a wreck, we marvel why
    The demon and its slaves can still be glad.

A PRAYER

Why mockest me, thou dearest, loveliest Muse?
  When all my days I've sought thy jeweled shrine,
  To offer there this heart and soul of mine,
  How canst thou still thy countenance refuse?
Wouldst thou but grant thy favor, I should choose
  No other worship saving only thine,
  Till blest by thee my song, thus made divine,
  Might rise to music it could never lose.
My foolish clamor beats itself in vain
  Upon the rock of thy unyielding breast,
  And dies away in inarticulate moan.
I chide thee not; but oh, let live the strain
  Which in my being ever unexpressed
  Still keeps me better than a desert stone.

Endure, thou fainting soul, thou must endure:
  Though thou hast labored and hast met but scath;
  Though baseness sicken thee; though Fortune's wrath
  Should rack and rend thee past all hope of cure,
And Love should feign herself too stripped and poor
  To help or bless, until at last it seems
  That Death should end thy unresultive dreams,
  Even then, despairing soul, thou shouldst endure;—
For lo, behold! all fellows are thy kin
  From mightiest sun to merest atomy;
  Yea, all that is, which shall be, and has been,
In that mysterious, vast immensity
  In which 'tis given thee to play thy part—
  Then forward, with fresh courage in thy heart!

Pine not, nor fret:
The rains will fall,
The sun will shine,
The flowers all bloom,
And grains and fruits
Their riches yield;
The wheels will turn,
And ever turn,
And ships still sail,
And ever sail.
But do thy part,
With faith and love,
As best thou canst,
And nought on earth
Can work thee ill,
Or make thee feel
One pang of fear.

BEATITUDE

TO J. A. Q.

Thrice blest is he, who, when Death comes
To bear him captive to the unknown realm,
Which lies beyond the reach of mortal ken,
Can look serenely in his awful face,
And hear the summons with complacent smile;
Who, looking back upon his earthly years,
Can see the trees of never-fading green,
Which flourish from the seeds, he planted, of good
       deeds;
And who, with blessing on the ones he loved,
And those who loved him in his worldly walks,
Where he dispensed the goodness of his heart,
Can look his last farewell without a sigh,
And fall asleep as peacefully as does
A wearied child upon its mother's breast.

On Nature's Breast

" My heart leaps up when I behold
   A rainbow in the sky;
So was it when my life began;
So is it now I am a man;
So be it when I shall grow old,
   Or let me die ! ''

WORDSWORTH.

" Underfoot the divine soil, overhead the sun.''

WALT WHITMAN.

NATURE'S CARE OF HER OWN

TO J. M. AND T. M.

Nature takes loving thought of all her own
　With marvellous cunning and with watchful eye,
　So that her countless brood may multiply,
　Nor leave their mother desolate and lone.
To the wild fruits by care of man unknown,
　That ripe where winter at his stormiest blows,
　She gives more seeds and better than to those
　In cultured garden delicately grown.
And so in him that on the rugged breast
　Of mountain finds his joy and his repose,
　Who makes the pine his fellow, and with zest
Treads the great glaciers and their kindred snows,
　A strength is planted that in direst test
　Dares all the devils of Danger to oppose.

45

Thou beckonest to me and I come once more;
 Once more to lay my head upon thy breast,
 And feel thy easeful, all-sufficing rest
 Body and mind deliciously steal o'er.
My soul so hungers for thy bounteous store,
 That every heart-beat of its riches sings,
 And every thought, on love's unflagging wings,
 Leaves far behind the city's maddening roar.
'Twere joy enough to have thee once again,
 If such possession were my very last
 This side of death: to leave the haunts of men,
And in thy solitudes, bespeaking vast,
 Entrancing mysteries, to be as one
 With sons and stars and all they look upon.

AT THE PRESIDIO OF SAN FRANCISCO

The rose and honeysuckle here entwine
  In lovely comradeship their amorous arms;
  Here grasses spread their undecaying charms,
  And every wall is eloquent with vine;
Far-reaching avenues make beckoning sign,
  And as we stroll along their tree-lined way,
  The songster trills his rapture-breathing lay
  From where he finds inviolable shrine.
And yet, within this beauty-haunted place
  War keeps his dreadful engines at command,
  With scarce a smile upon his frowning face,
And ever ready, unrelaxing hand . . .
  We start to see, when dreaming in these bowers,
  A tiger sleeping on a bed of flowers.

THE JONQUIL

TO W. B. K.

As o'er the city's dark and bustling street
  He swiftly made his task-appointed way,
  Before his feet upon the pavement lay
  The mute, appealing face of jonquil sweet—
No more its father Sun at morn to greet
  With music from its golden trumpet blown;
  Untimely plucked to perish all alone,
  Nor find in natal soil its winding sheet.
With tenderness he took the beauteous thing
  As yet unstained with soilure of the town,
  And for his friend he bade its music flow;
And now again in glory it doth ring,
  With note that gives it more than mortal crown,
  Of friendship blooming in the long ago.

BEAUTY

THE MAN TO THE ROSE:

O Rose, with heart of flaming gold,
Wilt tell me what thou hast been told,
And make me merry, make me sad,
With what thou knowest of good and bad?

I see thee bending lowly now
As if with weight of prayerful vow—
So lovely that I faint to see
The beauty glorified in thee;

But doubt will work its cruel way
Though fiend or angel bid it stay,
And now despite thy joy to me,
I fain would dare to question thee.

THE ROSE TO THE MAN:

Dost see the bee that gently sips
The nectar from my welcome lips?
He takes his good without a sigh,
Nor seems to seek for reason why.

My lover Sun I do not ask
For any but affection's task,

Beauty   Content to have him shine on me,
And breed the gold that puzzles thee.

But this I give for future thought:
When thou to me in love hast brought
Goodness and Truth, thou then mayst know
Why I and all my kind do blow.

AFTER THE STORM

The storm is o'er; the angry clouds
    All sullenly retire
To where beneath the western sun
    They blaze with peaceful fire;

While winds, that tore like demons wild
    At earth's defenceless breast,
Have sated their unwonted rage,
    And calmly sink to rest.

And now the grass looks up and laughs,
    And in the rose's heart,
Erst bowed with grief, I see a joy
    That heals my bosom's smart.

NIGHT

As oft of old, I watched the sun leap o'er
   The golden barriers of the farthest West,
   And saw the stars on heaven's deep azure breast
   In splendor blaze as never seen before;
And then upon mine ear began to pour,
   In waves innumerous that knew no rest,
   The sharp, sweet notes of myriad ones that blest
   My inmost soul with more than music's lore:
Unnoted these great stars glow all the day,
   Unheard these tiny insects chirp their lay—
   Eclipsed by louder sound, by brighter light.
Thus many a sweet and patient one of earth
   Shines on, sings on, unmarked her priceless worth
   Till she has glorified Misfortune's night.

AT DEL MONTE, CALIFORNIA
JULY 24, 1898.

TO M. E. OF CAMBRIDGE, ENGLAND.

We passed through hoary, dozing Monterey,
  And thrilled to see the gloried spot from where
  The Stars and Stripes first floated on the air,
  To give this matchless land a newer day;
Then through the piney woods we took our way,
  On either hand great ferns, the tangled hair
  Of varicolored vines, and blossoms fair
  That on earth's tawny breast all starlike lay.
And still we went until against the sky,
  Where hung the gray-hued banners of the mist,
  The weird, gnarled cypresses dazed sense and eye.
The shore was there by emerald breakers kissed;
  But from their crested bloom and sovran pride
  I turned to rose of England by my side.

ON SOME LANDSCAPES PAINTED BY
WILLIAM KEITH

I

Behold this canvas where the artist shows
   Our Golden Heritage: The sovran Sun
   In ripened harvest sees his triumph won,
   And golden glories deepen to repose,
Save where the laden wain an accent throws
   Of voiceful toil; afar the mountains swim;
   Great trees ensentinel the valley's rim,
   And childhood gambols where the streamlet flows.
O children, nature here has given her best—
   So rich, no poet could its wealth proclaim
   Though dowered with words of ruby-hearted flame;
Knead with it best of yours; and so possessed,
   May you, faced starward, mount to summits where
   Your souls shall blossom in celestial air.

The Golden Heritage of the Native Sons

The
Joy of
Earth

Who doubts the earth speaks audibly unto
    The heart of everyone that lists to hear,
    Setting its beats to music? If to thee not clear
    Her ceaseless note that rings beneath the blue;
Or hast thou never been impelled to woo
    Her beauty-glowing forms, nor sought her ways,
    I pray thee on this breathing picture gaze,
    That Art may give thee all thy soul's best due.
For here Earth seems with radiant joy to say:
    Behold the children born in love to me—
    These lush, deep grasses where the flowerets play
At hide and seek; this wide-embracing tree,
    Where birds may live their little, tuneful day,
    And golden harvests that are yet to be.

Full many a time fair April have I seen   *April*
   Enwrapped in cloud of every lovely hue,
   With tears that fell as soft as morning dew
   On bloomy orchard and on fields of green;
And watched her smilingly, her tears between,
   The balmy air with sun-born jewels strew,
   Till life and joy and song seemed born anew,
   To glorify with promise all the scene.
These, and still more, O Master, hast thou caught
   Within the meshes of thy subtile art,
   That April there, with quickening beauties fraught,
Might stir the languid waters of the heart,
   And make forever there all seasons hers
   To bid fulfilment crown the laboring years.

*The
Quiet
Wood*

Come with me into this all-quiet wood,
  Where nought of hurry or of noise is known,
  And where soft airs from every tree are blown,
To fill the heart with Rest's untroubled good.
Here we may lie on leaf-strown couch, and brood,
  While sweet Imagination binds her zone
  Around our vagrant thoughts, and stirs alone
The silence of this lovely solitude.
Thou precious Art! be always thus, so we
  May compass something of thy priceless lore:
  Thy deeper truths shall set the spirit free,
When soulless imitation rules no more,
  And where, as here, thy joyous liberty
  Gives birth to beauty never seen before.

To-day the soaring mount is not for me
   Though it should marshal all its loveliest mass,
   Or though across my tempted vision pass
   Its utmost witchery of rock and tree ;
For this lush meadow holds my heart in fee,
   Where clouds lie sleeping in its pool's clear glass,
   And where in comradeship with flower and grass
   No other friend than Reverie shall be.
The Mountain trumpets with imperious voice,
   And great Ambition sits enthronèd there
   With spoils that blaze in fever-laden air ;
But thou, sweet Meadow, bidst the soul rejoice
   In love of lowly and familiar things,
   And lead'st to peace's cooling, crystal springs.

The Meadow

The Enchanted Wood

With moss-grown, interlocking arms that wear
A beauty strangely true, these gnarlèd trees
Rule o'er this weird demesne, where mysteries
Seem lurking nigh in many an eerie lair.
Silence has closed the lips of every air,
Till hushful Rest, as though on drowsy seas,
Floats dreaming, safe from all disease
Of vain ambition or of mad despair.
To some such spot as this lone Dante might
Have brought the travail of his towering soul,
When exile's grief had made it joy to die;
And here Imagination, love-bedight,
Will over us its waves enchanted roll,
As near this naiad-haunted pool we lie.

The mild, alluring Night has had her time,   *Dawn*

   For now the Sun on his resistless way

   Beats down with mighty hand her vast array,

   And grandly up the heavens begins to climb.

These pulsing clouds announce the King sublime;

   Yet not with banner blazed with ruby ray,

   But one whose opal light of lustrous gray

   Wakes Dawn's sweet bells to silver-sounding chime.

The birds have scarce aroused, yet man is here,

   To lay the dewy grass beneath his knife

   And bear it off upon the waiting wain.

Thou wondrous New-born Day; what hope, what fear,

   Lie coiled within thy breast; what peace, what strife,

   And what ambitions that are worse than vain!

At
Twilight
Time

The Sun that raged victorious through the day,

    Like conquering monarch scornful of defeat,

    Behind the hills in unrestrained retreat

With pauseless haste now speeds upon his way.

He conquers still : these clouds proclaim his sway,

    That lace refulgently the lucent blue,

    And this lone-wandering moon with crescent new

Begins to glow with his reflected ray.

The grasses tanned by summer's breath, the trees,

    The distant crag a battlement that seems,

    Lie in the arms of silence and of rest.

The feverous day is done ; night's galaxies

    Hold yet aloof; in this mid-time what dreams

    May hover o'er us that shall make us blest !

In centre of the canvas see this pine

   All stark in death, with arms in vain appeal

   For what it nevermore can taste or feel

   Of joys of earth or of the heavens divine.

Straight as in life it stands, still bearing sign

   Of noble majesty and dauntless will;

   While at its base its elder brothers spill

   Their ashes where the grasses kiss and twine.

A glorious redwood centuries have blessed

   Uptowers, while with bliss of life possessed

   The forest sings in grand, harmonious tone.

And careless men pass by—the children they

   Of other children death has made his own,

   And who like them will strive and pass away.

*The
Unceasing
Round*

X

The
Dying
Year

The year is on the edge of death ; for see,
　These dreary branches have already shed
　Such myriad leaves, they lie in mounds of dead
　At foot of each sad-hearted parent tree.
Yet, grim and stern as human soul might be,
　The scarred, gray sycamores with defiant head
　Like warriors stand, while in its shrunken bed
　The languid stream flows on resignedly.
Life is aweary and in quiet here
　Would rest awhile her fever-haunted brain,
　As dreams she of the dear, departing year;
And Melancholy, led by Memory's train,
　With velvet step will gently come anear,
　To dew the ground with sacramental tear.

Behold : dark, lead-like clouds made beautiful
   With various forms of fantasy, where light
   Breaks through their lowermost edge with forceful
      might,
   As if in challenge of their right to rule;
Two birds that fly above a sleeping pool
   Wherein a woman peers with aching sight,
   While tree and grass, in mystic garment dight,
   Rest in the silence of a dreamful lull.
O Woman ! tell me what thou findest here
   In light and dark, in water, bird and tree,
   In all these grasses and their mystery.
O Man ! I am as thou : for could I peer
   Till Time made peace with Death, as now I do,
   No ray would show me the unraveling clew.

The
Fruitless
Quest

Promise The shower has ceased, yet big with coming rain
　　　　The light-fringed clouds loom o'er the gladsome hills,
　　　　While all the sunbeam-glinted valley thrills
　　　　With expectation of its harvest grain.
　　This fresh, sweet soil but just upturned is fain
　　　　Its seed to press; the orchard blossom spills
　　　　Its fragrance round; and rising incense fills
　　　　The air to gratitude's symphonic strain.
　　O Earth, dear, bounteous mother of us all,
　　　　From thee we come, and at the last we fall
　　　　Into thy softly folding arms to rest;
　　And as the Master spreads thy beauties here,
　　　　We seem to lie serenely on thy breast,
　　　　With Promise gently soothing every fear.

In Humble Praise

" He, above the rest
In shape and gesture proudly eminent,
Stood like a tower."

Paradise Lost, Book I, line 589.

" The Poet is the only potentate ;
    His sceptre reaches o'er remotest zones ;
    His thought remembered and his golden tones
Shall, in the ears of nations uncreate,
    Roll on for ages and reverberate
    When Kings are dust beside forgotten thrones."

Sestet of " The Sovereigns."—LLOYD MIFFLIN.

How glow they evermore, serenely bright,
These star-eyed ones—the immortal Sons of Light !

TO SHAKESPEARE

JUNE, 1898.

"As Carlyle said, we are all subjects of King Shakespeare. As long as the Americans acknowledge that allegiance, and in truth none could be more loyal, there can be no doubt as to their Englishry."

The Spectator, April 30, 1898

Why add superfluous, piping note of mine

    To those which for these now three hundred years

    Have sung thy name, that in transplendence rears

    Itself above the mightiest of thy line?

Why should I not, like nun before a shrine,

    Midst adoration's more than grateful tears,

    Let silence speak,* until the rapt soul hears

    The distant music of the shores divine?

Because in this tremendous time of throes,

    When all the lands are bowed with many woes,

    We joy to feel old England's hand in ours;

And so to-day, beyond imagining,

    We kneel, as thrilled with newly-wakened powers,

    Before thee—England's and our Country's King.

*" The holy time is quiet as a Nun
Breathless with adoration."—WORDSWORTH.

TO MILTON

Thou star-crowned, peerless Milton, thine to know
   The moans and thunders of the surging seas,
   The tinkling laugh of rippling rills, the trees'
   Soft murmurs multidudinous; and so
To make thy numbers with their music flow
   In such deep roll of cadenced harmonies,
   Such rythmic trip of honeyed melodies,
   That round the world forevermore they go.
Thy thoughts were high as heaven, as deep as hell,
   Strong as the truth, as sweet as liberty,
   And pure as thine own song of chastity.
Thou gavest England, when she needed well
   Her kingliest and her best, one rarest man
   Who grandly blended Greek with Puritan.

God built thee on the noblest plan,
Thou universal, matchless man!
No life there was thou couldst not feel,
Nor learning thou didst not acquire,
And these thine art did so anneal
They glow as with divinest fire.
Thy serious soul surveyed the all,
Contemning not what seemed the small,
Nor lost in mazes of the vast;
While all thy years thou wisely wast
The conqueror of thyself, who could
Dispart the evil from the good,
And calmly sit above the show
Of froth and fume that raged below.
Thou sat'st on an imperial throne,
Making all forms of life thine own—
A mighty, intellectual force,
Appointing man his proper course.
Thy piercing vision saw the springs
That lie within the heart of things,

And thy enthralling voice shall sound
Its notes to earth's remotest bound,
To lift mankind on eagle's wings
To where sweet Peace in triumph sings.

TO MATTHEW ARNOLD

Clear-sighted and clear-thoughted, thou ;
Dogmatic, as we must allow ;
But temperate alway and sincere,
And void of bias as of fear.

So limpid thy prosaic flow,
We could with thee forever go,
To catch the rich and rare delight
Of seeing clearness joined to might.

And with thy verse we breathe an air
The very Gods would wish to share,
Where passion linked with beauty glows
Mid restful calms of great repose.

Here was a Titan:—one whose teeming thought
  In unfamiliar channels, broad and deep,
  Rolled on with seeming superhuman sweep;
  One who, by learning as by nature taught,
In every mine of human passion wrought
  With such exhaustless power, such piercing ken,
  Such boundless sympathy, as poet's pen,
  Save his and matchless Shakespeare's, never caught.
One who met truth with never flinching gaze,
  As on he walked with Muse for loving guide;
  Who kept his road, despite of blame or praise,
In fiercest scorn of intellectual pride;
  And who, at close of his unrivalled days,
  Sleeps, where 'tis meet he should, by Chaucer's side.

TO BALZAC,
ON READING HIS MEMOIR BY
MISS WORMELEY

Until I knew the story of thy years,
    It did not seem titanic power like thine
    Could have been found in merely human mine,
    Or could have mingled with life's hopes and fears;
For thy great spirit so sublime appears
    Among the kindred fellows of thy line,
    That all the Nine would hail thee as divine,
    And Atropos for once distrust her shears.
'Tis so set down, yet strange I feel it still,
    That thou wast not the demi-god I deemed,
    But anxious toiler for thy daily bread;
Thy bosom racked with many a torturing ill;
    And who, like others, when thy dreams were dreamed,
    Saw Death's dark angel cloud thy helpless head.

TO JOSÉ-MARIA DE HEREDIA

'Twas eagle-winged, imperial Pindar who
    Sent down the ages on the tide of song
    The thought that only to the years belong
    Those deeds that win immortal poet's due.
Still rise his crownèd athletes to the view,
    On his unwearied pinions borne along;
    Still shepherd's pipe and lay sound sweet and strong
    As when Theocritus attuned them true.
And so through thee the feats of heroes great,
    The hues of life of other times than ours,
    With such refulgence in thy sonnets glow,
That in the splendor of their new estate,
    They there, with deathless Art's supernal powers,
    Shall o'er the centuries enchantments throw.

TO CARLYLE

Thou strangest one of lettered men,
Whose scathing tongue and piercing pen
No mercy had for vain pretense,
Thou mov'st us less with love than awe;
Yet no one could before thee draw
Without enlargement of his sense;
Without sensations such as ne'er
Before had stirred his spirit's air;
Without conviction, too, that here
Was one who dared to be sincere—
A stern, unflinching soul, whose blow
Spared neither self, nor friend, nor foe.
A Prophet, thou, who strov'st to teach
The deepest truths mankind can reach;
Who knew not what it was to try
To compromise with any lie,
Whate'er might threaten or beseech;
And whose unwonted, thunderous speech
Will furnish man with generous store
Till Earth and Time shall be no more.

ON LOOKING AT WORDSWORTH'S ENGRAVED PICTURE IN THE CENTEN-ARY EDITION OF HIS POEMS

Immortal Wordsworth, as thy pictured face,
  With all its placid calm, its brow serene,
  Its mild, benignant majesty of mien,
  Moves me to-day as with unwonted grace,
I fain would yield, if only for a space,
  My soul to thee completely, and so clean
  My thoughts of all impurities terrene,
  That they with thine might dare to interlace.
Thou glorious singer of soul-quickening song;
  Thou nature's child to being's very core;
  Simple in all thy ways, yet bold and strong;
One that to loftiest mountain-top could soar
  With sweeping wing, and lightly skim along,
  No less at ease, the valley's daisied floor.

TO BYRON

Byron, volcanic soul, whose crater's fire
    Gushed without pause in heart-consuming pain,
    The world still owns the brilliance of thy reign,
    And wreathes with amaranth that throbbing lyre,
Where passion cries in unappeased desire,
    Where nature pulsates in her every vein,
    Where lofty thought evokes its loftiest strain,
    And scorn of cant is hot with scourging ire.
As restless thou and ample as the sea
    That sported with thee as familiar friend;
    Thy heart was open, and thy spirit free
Beyond all human power to break or bend;
    Thy face was starward set, and Liberty
    Wept with mankind at thy untimely end.

TO KEATS

I

Dear Keats, forgive me that I cannot fly
   The sweet temptation of a verse to thee,
   Whose name, deep writ in brass, shall ever be
   Still deeper written as the years go by;
But looking in that tender, haunting eye
   Which Severn drew for men to fondly see,
   Thou dost to-day so radiant seem to me,
   That love extorts what prudence might deny.
'Tis not alone the glories of thy song,
   Nor thy young death (at which mankind still weeps),
   That binds us closely to thee, but thy strong,
Enduring steadfastness as well, which keeps
   The golden glories of thy precious name
   Secure within our hearts a vestal flame.

II

*To
Keats*

Thou art, indeed, of all the poet race
   The Muses' most immediate, darling child;
   They kissed thee at thy birth and fondly smiled,
   Foreseeing what thy splendors would embrace:
Enchantments man would never cease to chase,
   And catch and catch again, and be beguiled,
   Till filled with rapture he should be so isled
   Upon such sparkling sea of fairy space.
Thou clear-eyed soul! Thou miracle of song!
   Greek and Elizabethan met in thee;
   Thy honeyed lips all beauteous things did throng,
Attuned to music's noblest ecstasy,
   Making thy world so ravishingly fair,
   That all the years shall rest delighted there.

TO TENNYSON

As comes to all, so thou hast passed away
  To that unfathomable, dark beyond,
  Before whose mysteries thine enchanting wand
  Stirred soulful music to her deepest play ;
And meet it was that when Death came, to lay
  His icy finger on that dreamful brain,
  Thy soul should yearn for Shakespeare's choric strain
  To fill the moments of thy parting day.
Thou deftest master of poetic art,
  Whose verse is tinct with noble dignity,
  And makes of England an immortal part !
Familiar things are glorified by thee,
  While dullest blood leaps lightly through the heart
  At thy immatchless song of chivalry.

Of all the poets never yet was one
More blest by fortune than was Tennyson:
For half a century his pen so swayed
The realm of Poesy that all obeyed,
And owned he gave such jeweled song-words birth
As could not well be matched upon the earth.
His country held him closely to her breast
As one in whom she was uniquely blest,
While wife, and friends, and children, all were his,
And spoils of wealth and noble dignities.
He dreamed his dreams in quietude apart,
His every passion centring in his art,
And from his garden's uninvaded shade
In calm contentment all the world surveyed,
Keeping his powers in such consummate bloom
They never seemed to wither or to fade.
And when had come the fateful hour of doom,
Good fortune still was his: the moonbeams made
Transfiguring beauty of his chamber's gloom;

The Master's music lingered on his lips

The latest ere his spirit passed away,

And sudden sunlight burst through cloud's eclipse

In golden glory on his coffined clay.

TO BURNS

Thou wast of truest flesh and blood :

Thy veins ran hot with passion's flood ;

Thou knewest the stars—and miry mud—

    But all sincerely ;

And so the world, as well it should,

    Loves thee most dearly.

All nature's kin was kin of thine ;

The earth for thee was all divine ;

Nor needest thou from Heaven a sign

    To love thy brothers,

Nor wouldst thou measure with thy line

    The faults of others.

'Tis true thy satire's lash did smite

The tender spot of many a wight ;

But though thy blow was never light,
    It meant no evil;
Indeed, thou didst not do despite
    E'en to the Devil.

And yet thy bosom nursed a hate
For bigotry that would not bate;
For aught that bound thy fellow's fate
    To tyrant burdens,
Or barred him from his just estate
    Of worthy guerdons.

The lowliest ones that breathe the air
Could catch thy thought and feel thy care,
And nestling in thy heart find there
    Unselfish giver,
Till winged with song their flight shall bear
    Still on forever.

Thy artless strain, how rich and strong!
How full of all the joys of song!
How round the heart its children throng
    To leave us never!
How scornful of the meanly wrong,
    Yet loving ever!

Why should we note thy fitful years,
Remorseful pangs, repentant tears,

Or sigh that Fate had used her shears

    Untimely on thee?

'Tis nought, when blessed Love appears

    Fore'er to crown thee.

TO WALTER SAVAGE LANDOR

Landor, thou art, in truth, the one unique:

A Briton, yet a Roman and a Greek,

And still no less Italian; in all time

Breathing ambrosial airs of every clime;

Who all the spoils of all the ages stored,

And drew such honey from thy heaping hoard,

That we who read thee pause and pause again

In wonder at the marvels of thy pen.

A lettered Titan, thou, so greatly great,

Thou sittest throned in high imperial state,

Like some immortal God that keeps his place

In lonely grandeur of unconquered space,

With none so venturesome as dare dispute

His rule as being less than absolute.

Dear Goldsmith, how we dwell and gloat
Upon thy clear and liquid note,
And with thy Vicar talk until
Sweet Resignation leads the will.
Thy Traveller still pursues his way;
Thy Village glows in its decay
More lovely now than when it first
Upon the world of letters burst;
Thy Citizen still makes us hear;
Thy Bee still buzzes in our ear;
Still does thy conquering Lady show
The self-same charms of long ago;
While Garrick and Sir Joshua stand
Forever painted by thy hand.

  Who could have thought, of all the set
With Johnson at the Turk's-head met,
That thou shouldst be the one bright star
Whose light eclipse should never bar;
That thy belovèd name should trail
The rest behind thee like a tail?

TO CHARLES LAMB

'Tis three score years, dear Lamb, since thou
Tasted the bitter and the sweet of death,
But Love thy name hath nurtured so, that now,
As ne'er before, it greenly flourisheth.
Thou hadst sincerity without a flaw,
And lovedst all so deeply and so true,
Thou to the beggar and the sweep couldst draw,
And see their hearts their rags and tatters through.
Thou hadst no theories for wayward man,
Nor sought to teach some lesson to thy kind,
But livedst patiently thy little span,
To hopeless ills courageously resigned.
    Thy writings leave us debtors evermore,
    But what thou wast makes still the richer store.

If highest taste some *Songs* of thine would blot,
 Thy *Drama* raises its Olympian head
 Above our wonder.—All divinely fed
 With the ambrosia of enkindling thought
And soul-enthralling music, and inwrought
 With rarest beads of color-laden phrase,
 It grandly moves in such heroic ways
 As scarce one modern, saving thee, has sought.
Here Scotland's Mary winds through her career,
 Her dainty fingers dipped in every crime;
 Here Knox, the dauntless, shakes his priestly spear;
Here Bothwell schemes, the Satan of his time,
 And here antiquity has been rewon
 Through Atalanta's chase in Calydon.

ON LOOKING INTO THE POEMS OF
WILLIAM ERNEST HENLEY

What sweep of wing !—what moving power !—
What strange, inevitable things
That menacingly loom and lower,
  Bodeful and big with doom !

No puny morbidness here broods,
But thoughts and words of giant form
That stride across the vastitudes
  In color-glinted gloom.

He holds us fast, and binds the will
So closely round our inmost thought,
We feel an unaccustomed thrill
  To ecstasy akin.

The Hospital its story sings
Through every gamut of the strain,
And London, gloomed and glorious, brings
  Her terror and her sin.

All nature throbs with strange desire,
While themes deemed barren or outworn

Burst from his music-haunted lyre
  In blooms of kingliest line.

Too lurid, lacking sober rest,
Some critic cries—and let him cry ;
For here are gems, with beauty blest,
  From Art's eternal mine.

TO RUSKIN

WRITTEN IN "ARROWS OF THE CHACE."

Thou noble one, thy mind and heart
  We reverence more the more we scan,
The more we see thy love for Art
  Moves hand in hand with love for Man.

TO WILLIAM BLAKE

Thou strange, rare one, with spirit free,
What glorious visions didst thou see ;
How teach us that the truest Real
Is that contained in the Ideal.

CHRISTOPHER SMART

Smart was the marvel of his sapless time :
To scribble reams of empty, futile rhyme,
Then in a phrensy of poetic art—
Crazed in his brain and saddened in his heart—
To pour his soul into one mighty song,
Where sparkling jewels do so thickly throng,
And blaze with such imaginative light,
That every year shall gladden in their sight—
A deathless song with nature's ruin bought ;
No wonder his own century knew him not!

TO WILLIAM WATSON

Thou dost the verses of thy brethren praise
In rarest nicety of tuneful phrase,
But who, all gladdened with Parnassian wine,
Will sing the crystal purity of thine?

TO JAMES RUSSELL LOWELL

AUGUST 12, 1891.

Lowell, thou art not dead; thou canst not die
   Till Letters' children all shall cease to be;
   Till dawns the day (but who such day may see?)
   When Art's innumerous crystal springs run dry;
When Fancy skims no more the meads that lie
   In fadeless bloom, and doomed by death's decree
   Imagination's mighty majesty.
   Till then, O glorious soul, thou shalt not die.
Thou art the perfectest of all the flowers
   That yet have blossomed on New England's soil—
   Blending great character with stintless powers,
And making every literature thy spoil;
   While all thy years thy jewel-crusted pen
   Sent thrilling message to the hearts of men.

Could I but mount with something of thine ease,
　　And lightly wing the empyreal air
　　The muses breathe, I would not now despair
　　To rise in praise of thee on lines like these;—
Now, when thy dulcet, fine felicities
　　All freshly lie upon my soul, and wear
　　A bloom so richly, beautifully fair,
　　They mock expression's subtlest alchemies.
No deliration ever mars thy strain,
　　No puling,　weak complaining nor lament,
　　Nor hobbling verse that roughly drags along;
But borne on waves of music, sweetly sane,
　　Serenely passioned, suavely eloquent,
　　It glows with witching art of noble song.

ON THE LYRICS OF THOMAS BAILEY ALDRICH

Dainty as daintiest thing
In man's imagining
Of words that faultless fit
Their fabric exquisite;
With beauty such as rose
In happiest moment knows;
Attuned to melody's
Supremest ecstasies;
These gemlike lyrics live through flawless art,
To please the senses and to stir the heart.

POPE

The choicest vintage of ambrosial wine
He knew not, nor the harmonies divine;
But who has matched, or who shall hope to match,
The wit and sparkle of his rapier line?

TO WILLIAM CULLEN BRYANT

Thou wast of those who lived with noble things
From very birth, until, weighed down with years,
Death sealed thine eyes, whilst all thy country stood
Uncovered round thy venerated clay.
'Twas thine to show how clean the Press could be,
And how courageous; thine to clearly point
The paths thy countrymen might safely tread,
And what they ought in honor to acclaim;
And thine, in combat for a purer tongue,
To bid thine own example lead the way
In very panoply of chastest mail.
The gift of song was thine; and in thy great
Miltonic cadences the mighty heart
Of nature beats, anon with joy serene,
Anon with melancholy sad as leaves
By Autumn kissed, but alway with a hope
That sings its music to the darkest hour.
With thee we lose ourselves within the wood,
And make the tree our brother; every plant,
That spreads its modest beauties to the sun,
Or nestles in the shade, is then our kin,

And we with them on nature's kindly breast

In silence hearken to the voice divine.

The flowers of the field were thy dear friends,

Who spake their message to thee as to one

They trusted ; and in swelling, golden note

Of sounding rhythm thou gavest it to us

To keep enshrined in love's own treasury.

All things that walk or fly could set thy soul

To harmony, as did the waterfowl

Which caught thine eye, when in the vast

Of space's unimaginable waste

Alone, yet confident, it took its way,

And where, through thee, transfigured and sublime,

It beats forever an unwearied wing.

POE

He walked beneath the raven's wing
  A wayward child in lightless gloom,
And there his trancing songs did sing
  And weave his haunting tales of doom.

He drank from Beauty's honey-cup,
  Pressed to his eager lips by Art,
Until her nectar swallowed up
  The very substance of his heart.

Upon her lines his structures grew,
  In form most cunningly designed,
While demons that he nurtured slew
  The peace and sweetness of his mind.

With hopeless sighs and bitter tears
  He filled his sad, remorseful hours,
Yet reared the while, for all the years,
  His beauty-crowned, enchanted towers.

TO LLOYD MIFFLIN

AFTER READING "AT THE GATES OF SONG."

Borne on thy sonnet-feathered wings I fly
   To strange, vast realms immeasurable where
   Imagination breeds her children fair,
   That wake, with singing, Thought's remotest sky.
Then down to earth thou bring'st me, and I lie
   So sweetly close to every human care,
   And breathe the joys of such ambrosial air,
   That Love's seraphic host seems hovering nigh.
Where'er thou bearest me all beauties bide
   With Art and Passion linked, while music rolls
   In cadenced billows on the spirit's shore.
O Poet by the Susquehanna's side,
   Take thou this heart-wrought song and all my soul's
   Most faithful homage till my days are o'er.

WRITTEN IN LLOYD MIFFLIN'S
"THE SLOPES OF HELICON"
APRIL 14, 1898.

Thou alien one, O War, whose notes prelude
  Full many a grievous woe to haughty Spain,
  Nor less, mayhap, to us, let not their bane
  On this glad day upon mine ear obtrude;
And thou familiar one, O Law, endued
  With that which should make battle's havoc vain,
  Must now release me from thy stress and strain,
  And leave my spirit to its solitude.
For now have come to me the lyric songs
  Of him whose numbers with impassioned might
  In beauty flow mellifluously on;
And hence this golden day to him belongs,
  On which he shall, with soul-illuming light,
  Lead me along the Slopes of Helicon.

97

TO WHITTIER

I

Some verse there is death cannot touch although
   It may not nest upon the loftiest height,
   To spread its pinions in untiring flight
   Where constellations in resplendence glow;
Nor yet by Fancy fondly fellowed know
   Her fairy realms of exquisite delight;
   Nor with Imagination's stopless might
   Range the vast regions of our bliss and woe;—
For it hath cradled in the human breast
   Feelings and thoughts with which we would not part;
   And hath in loving, saving strength possessed
The power to move the universal heart,
   And so will be by all the muses blest
   As long as joys shall sing, or tears shall start.

Such verse, O Whittier, thy muse employs:

   For thou dost sing in unaffected lay

   Of maidens fair, of childhood's glorious day,

   Of natural things unmixed with base alloys;

Dost mint the gold which lies in homely joys,

   And gently mov'st in such consummate way

   The human heartstrings to harmonious play,

   That restful music drowns the world's mad noise.

New England lives in thy delightful line:

   There do her household hearths our love constrain;

   There do her tales with newer beauty shine,

Her fields, her woods, her skies, her stormy main;

   While over all the Power we feel divine

   Upholds eternal, universal reign.

TO A SOILED AND BROKEN VOLUME OF
BAYARD TAYLOR'S POEMS

Come, lovely waif, to my embrace ;
With gentlest touch I shall erase
All soilure from thy pretty face,
Shall tear away the faded dress
That mars thy pristine loveliness,
And bid the binder clothe anew
Thy beauteous form, and there bestrew,
With hand by loving taste controlled,
His daintiest flowers of gleaming gold.
Then shall I gladly house thee where
The best of all thy kinsmen fare,
And who will give thee welcome room
Within the precints of their home,
And where thine author e'en would say
Thou hadst at last not gone astray.
There shalt thou have such tender care
The bitter past will be forgot ;
And oft to thee shall I repair,
To thrill beneath thy glowing thought ;
To follow thee at leisure times

For art-grown pearls in distant climes ;
To have the sluggish feelings stirred
By many a music-singing word,
And mount with thee on lyric wings
Above the touch of sordid things.
Ah, then how happy shall I be,
At thought of having rescued thee !

*To a
Soiled and
Broken
Volume of
Bayard
Taylor's
Poems*

TO FITZ-GREENE HALLECK

Thy verse, dear Halleck, hath such flowing ease,
And sparkles with such rare felicities ;
So much of it is nourished with a blood
That flows from sources of perennial good ;
We cannot still but wonder more and more
Thou shouldst have doled us such a stinted store ;
But every soul forgives thee when it turns
To read, for hundredth time, thy song to Burns.

TO WALT WHITMAN

Thou roughest-hewn of all the poet kind !—
   Not thine to tinkle rhyme's melodious bell,
   Nor set to music of harmonious swell
   The thoughts that surged within thy shoreless mind ;
Not these could Art to lightest durance bind,
   Nor sensuous Beauty with her deepest spell
   Entice them in her fair demesne to dwell ;
   But formless, ruleless they, as unconfined.
Yet, giant soul, thy loud-resounding lyre,
   Whose tones the wondering world still leans to hear,
   Thrills every spirit that would dare to be
Inflamed with that unique, immortal fire,
   That made thee what thou wast—the grandest seer
   And noblest poet of Democracy.

TO GEORGE FREDERICK WATTS, R. A.

ON HIS EIGHTIETH BIRTHDAY
FEBRUARY 23, 1897.

No worthier, nobler name, great Watts, than thine
  Has Art emblazoned on her golden scroll;
  Nor has old England gendered truer soul
  Of all the wonders of her wondrous line:
For thou hast borne with marvellous strength the sign
  Of Beauty's chastity to highest goal,
  Unheeding largess of applause or dole,
  Nor taking thought in worldly ways to shine.
And all the while Imagination's hand
  Has led thee to the unclouded summits, where
  For souls like thine all high ideals await—
Those radiant ones that spurn each base demand
  Of fad or falseness, and in Truth's pure air
  Teach what it means to be supremely great.

In Tribute

"I cannot love thee as I ought,
    For love reflects the thing beloved;
    My words are only words, and moved
Upon the topmost froth of thought."

                                    In Memoriam.

Trifles that glittered in affection's sun,
    Then passed like morning dew,
And which through eloquence of love have won
    The right to live anew.

A. S. T.

So deep her love, so warm her heart, her touch
So soft and gentle, and her voice so sweet,
That when she soothes my pain, then overmuch
My life seems blest; and thus serene, complete,
By means of her, my soul can never meet
One danger that shall make it cower or retreat.

TO PROFESSOR JACOB COOPER, D. D., D. C. L., OF RUTGERS COLLEGE, NEW JERSEY

I have not seen the nobleness and grace
That surely sit in glory on thy face,
For never has it been my joy to know
Thy spoken word in golden, friendly flow;
But many a token have I had from thee
So rarely sweet and beautiful to see,
And have so gazed upon thy distant light,
That in thy modesty's supreme despite
I give thee homage in this verse of mine,
And sigh to think I lack the Muse's might
To make it thrill with all that is divine.

TO Dr. LEVI COOPER LANE ON THE OPENING OF LANE HOSPITAL

JANUARY 1, 1895.

" Finis Coronat Opus."

I

Unconquerable soul, as fortunate
  As good and true, and worthy all the store
  That binds our hearts to thine still more and more,
  We bring thee loving homage on this great,
Auspicious day, yet vainly strive to mate
  Our feelings with the best of every lore,
  That bodied thus they might superbly soar
  On golden, wingèd words to Heaven's own gate.
Here stands thy work, and shall forever stand
  As long as man may know disease or pain,
  In flawless roundness of completion planned ;—
What nobler monument of selfless gain !
  In all that's precious, how supremely grand
  This wise creation of thy heart and brain !

Long years ago thy prescient soul made bold

   To point to rich fruition such as this,

   And now thou drainest such a cup of bliss

   As even thyself couldst scarce have hoped to hold;

But every purpose of thy hard-earned gold

   Has been accomplished; nought has gone amiss,

   And all thy plans harmoniously kiss

   Here where thy name shall evermore be told.

The starry heights have been sublimely won,

   And we who watched thee on thy toilsome way

   Are thrilled to see the splendor of thy sun

Undimmed as yet by age, and fervent pray

   That as the years their future courses run,

   Their peace shall bless thee to thy latest day.

To
Dr. Levi
Cooper
Lane

Death holds our Curtis now;—no more that pen
   From which fell crystal drops of honeydew;
   No more that spoken word, so strong and true,
   For sweet refreshment of the souls of men.
Nor tongue, nor pen, will ever speak again
   This side of Heaven; but Fame will fondly strew
   His grave with amaranth, and Love renew
   Her passion there to utmost of her ken;
For he was more than Letters' honored child,
   And more than lover of the artist race:
   His country held him as her noble son
Who strove to make her parties undefiled,
   To lift their feet from out the filth of place,
   And set them where real victories might be won.

DAVID STARR JORDAN,
PRESIDENT OF LELAND STANFORD JUNIOR
UNIVERSITY

Six feet and more his massive figure stands,
  With countenance sedate, yet frankly free,
  And with calm mien so masterful that we
  Could fear no cause committed to his hands.
As one beloved by Science he commands
  Her largesses, and bids them bodied be
  In closely-woven speech wherein we see
  Inweaved all great ideals' bright golden strands.
Sincere, courageous, never less than bold
  In scorn of weakness and of compromise,
  He keeps straight on to where his duty lies;
In body, mind and soul so big of mould,
  That when the most of him is thought or told,
  He seems beyond us still to higher rise.

TO WILLIAM KEITH

O Master, if such halting verse as mine
   Can for a moment stay thy magic brush,
   Then let, mid thankfulness' religious hush,
   My grateful tribute fall on ear of thine.
Our friendship's years have stretched a hallowed line
   Since first I knew the children of thy Art,
   And now, with wider thought and warmer heart,
   I come my laurel round thy name to twine.
Would that my rhyme could run as does this stream
   Which on thy canvas breaks in rapturous song
   Where Spring, triumphant, bursts from every clod!
Then would be realized my vain, fond dream:
   To sing one bar that might amidst the throng
   Of countless voices rise from earth to God.

ON READING THE POSTHUMOUSLY PUB-LISHED VOLUME OF TIMOTHY H. REARDEN

'Tis strange to think I should have held his hand,—
    Full many a time all warmly clasped in mine,—
    And ne'er was conscious that he bore the sign
Of those who conquer by divine command.
And now he's gone, how well we understand;
    How gloat upon the once unnoted line ;
    How newly bright his gems of beauty shine,
As born to live in Art's enchanted land.
The Muses loved him, but the cruel Fates
    Held his high hopes in many a sad eclipse,
    And led his feet where guerdon could not be ;
But at the last, Heaven opened wide its gates
    To light him, and with song upon his lips
    He hailed the glory of the eternal sea.*

* His poem, " *The Sea! The Sea!*" was written a short
time before his death.

TO MY FRIEND W. H. T.

Friend of my struggling years, when friend was none,
　　Save only thou, to set my wavering feet
　　On paths where effort and reward should meet;
　　Whose blood and mine have mingled into one
Through fruitful marriage;—ere thy westering sun
　　Shall sink one second lower, let my verse
　　Thy merit and my gratitude rehearse,
　　And so live there when both our days are done:
In counsel wise, with scorn of useless speech,
　　Tenacious to the last, yet just to each,
　　And modest ever, this, and more, thou art;
While never man was born who starred his way
　　With more unselfish deeds from day to day,
　　Or nursed his feelings in a tenderer heart.

He, like some prophet in the days of old,
   Took every weary heart into his own,
   And sought assuagement of the dreadful moan
Forever rising and by nought controlled.
Against the giant wrongs whose coils enfold
   The myriad souls that starve, and freeze, and groan,
   His flaming message flew as if 'twere blown
By all the woes that earth has ever told.
His love was man's until his latest day,
   When, battling 'gainst corruption's foul array,
   He fell, to flood with glory all the scene.
Alas! Alas! the world has lost him now;
   But men will look to it that on his brow
   The laurel keeps imperishably green.

TO ANDRÉE'S CARRIER PIGEON

IN THE ARCTIC OCEAN, 80° 44′ NORTH, 20° 20′ EAST
JULY 16, 1897.

No voice but thine, O ill-requited bird,
   Has come to tell of mighty-souled Andrée,
   Since that uniquely memorable day
   His polar voyaging the whole world stirred ;
And as on sheltering mast—thy flight deterred
   By cold and weariness—thy body lay,
   Wrapped in the dreams of home-cote far away,
   Man gave thee death for thy recorded word.
Thy master sailed into the depths unknown
   Along the paths no human wing had beat,
   And fell with frozen plume, no more to rise ;
And twinned with thee ye both, as glory's own,
   Have added, with transplendency complete,
   New Borealis to the Arctic skies.

And so you're back from London town,
　From Paris and from Florence;
You've seen Italia's lovely plains,
　And Alpine peaks and torrents;

You've gloated over gems of art
　In many an olden city;
The Louvre and Luxembourg have walked,
　Uffizi and the Pitti;

You've racked your brain to find what's in
　Libraries and museums,
And various music heard, from pipe
　Of shepherd to *Te Deums.*

You've breathed the classic air of Greece
　That all mankind inspires,
And thrilled before the Parthenon's
　Unquenched, immortal fires,

And watched the witching moonlight kiss
　Each rent and mutilation,
Till all her columns seemed to rise
　In glad rejuvenation,

And once again her sculptured host
　In joyousness possessed her,
While great Athene shone as when
　The art of Phidias blessed her.

You've trod the streets which Plato trod,—
　In silent, dreaming wonder,
And climbed Hymettus where the bees
　The nectared blooms still plunder;

Thermopylæ has felt your step,
　And Marathon and Platæa,
Where Asia's fall made sure for us
　The priceless Greek idea;

And Salamis was yours to see,
　With all its memories glowing:—
The Persian monarch throned in state,
　To watch the battle's flowing;

Themistocles' heroic form
　Above his fellows towering,
The wives and children on the height
　In fear and wailing cowering;

The Asian host on Attic's shore
    The victory bespeaking;
The writhing ships, the valorous deeds,
    The sea with slaughter reeking,

Until the evening sun looked down
    On Persia wrecked and flying,
While Greece in glory flamed along
    New-splendored and undying.

Over the hills of mighty Rome
    And through her ways you've wandered,
And o'er her everlasting mark
    On history's page have pondered;

You've mused where Caracalla's baths
    Upon the ground lie sprawling,
Until Rome's grandeur and her shame
    From out the past were calling;

You've stood where Titus sat, when he
    The Colosseum's wonder
Opened with seas of blood that ran
    Below applause's thunder;

To
C. S. K.
And where the Forum's columns stand
  In splendid ruination,
You've conjured up the populace,
  The Tribune and oration;

You've bended o'er the fateful place
  Which Brutus made appalling,
Until in fancy you could see
  The towering Julius falling;

You've roamed the Vatican where Art
  Her vigil still is keeping,
And knelt upon the grave where Keats
  Immortally is sleeping;

You've read your Virgil mid the scenes
  Where sang the master classic,
And viewed the farm where Horace versed
  'Tween sips of fragrant Massic;

You've followed Dante's dauntless steps
  In exile from his city,
And Tasso's prison walls have felt
  The murmur of your pity.

You've gazed on Venice, sailed upon
  Her marvellous streets aquatic,
And lived the matchless scene when she
  Wedded the Adriatic;

And thought of all that far-gone time,
  When power was hers and glory,
Till every age entranced has heard
  Recital of her story;

When Dandolo, the sightless Doge,
  Joined arms with the crusader,
And far and near full many a land
  Submissively obeyed her;

When Tintoretto's brush was tinct
  With great imagination,
And Titian's and Giorgione's glowed
  With gorgeous coloration;

And when Manuzio raised his press,
  And with his slanting letters
Set free the Muses' royal line
  From manuscriptal fetters.

To
C. S. K.

Language you've mastered; bent your thought
  On problems of the nations,
And pondered o'er the mystic past,
  With all its vast relations;

And more, and more; but why recount
  When you are here before us,
To let narration's gentle waves
  Delightfully roll o'er us?

YSAŸE

All leonine in look he stands,
  Serious, confident, serene,
Whilst 'neath his supple, willowy hands
  His myriad-voicèd violin
Speaks to the soul, until the air
Seems tremulous with praise and prayer.

TO BONZIG

(SEE PARTS II AND IV OF "THE MARTIAN" BY
GEORGE DU MAURIER")

Thou honest soul, amidst the dry routine
   Where school-boys mocked thy mild severity,
   How thou didst feed thy hunger for the Sea
By painting her thine eyes had never seen.
And when thy years were turning from their green,
   Ecstatic thoughts of her still came to thee,
   As in thy garret on thy canvas she
Glowed as with jewels from her great demesne.
O rapturous day that makes thy heart run o'er!
   The Baron calls thee to the ocean-shore,
   And says thou shalt be tutor to his son . . .
Then as thou criest,—bliss in every breath,—
   "The Sea! the Sea! my best belovèd one!"
   Thou plungest in her waves . . . and findest death.

My father, plead no more;—wouldst have me wed
  Remorse in life, and then in flames to lie,
  When from the blood of Cæsar's circus I
  Can leap to Heaven to be chapleted?
Has not our holy Saint Ignatius said
  God's wheat we are, that, for his purpose high
  And in his boundless love, should be ground by
  The teeth of wild beasts into Christ's pure bread?
Then welcome the arena's glorious ruth;
  I long to feel the lion's rending tooth
  Till all my body reeks with horrors fell.
And yet, dear father, ere from thee I go,
  It touches me to think of that great woe
  Which will be thine eternally in Hell.

"I hear—and shake not—that thou art decreed
   By thine own hand to miserably die,
   Now when thy fortunes blossom and the eye
   Of fate beams bright as with prophetic meed ;
And why shak'st thou in this thy spirit's need
   When Death and Cæsar stand relentless by ?
   Arouse thy soul till thy defiant cry
   Proclaims once more our matchless Roman breed."—

" O wife, to close this day my book of years
   Is unimagined pain ; this waiting steel
   The horror's sum of horrors unto me."—

" Give me the blade, that so thy griefs and fears
   May drown in mine own blood.   I strike . . .
       and feel
   No hurt, my Pætus . . . now the point's for
       thee."

IN THE CONVENT GARDEN

TO EDWIN STEVENS IN APPRECIATION OF HIS RENDERING
OF THE CHARACTER OF CYRANO DE BERGERAC

Steeped in autumnal dyes the mournful leaves
  With sad insistence flutter to the ground,
  And blend their voices with the vespers' sound,
  To soothe the heart that still for Christian grieves.
Beneath the sighing trees her bosom heaves;
  For memories throng, while he that in her bound
  Brings worldly word comes not—he whom,
      thorn-crowned,
  She still, as ever, blindly misconceives.
At last all worn he comes with feeble breath,
  In whose sweet tenderness preluding death
  Throbs strangely new a note from love's past years:
It tells that he, not Christian, won her kiss,
  That his, not Christian's, pen had fed her bliss,
  And that Remorse shall fill her cup with tears.

HARRO

SCHLESWIG-HOLSTEIN COAST,
FEBRUARY, 1895.

The waves leapt fierce and high
Beneath cloud-blackened sky,
And raging winds tore by
    The ship that staggered on,
While blinding sleet fell there,
From out the freezing air,
Upon her bosom where
    Hope seemed forever gone.

And now the seas dash o'er
Her deck's defenseless floor,
And more and ever more
    She gasps and pants for breath;
While, worn with weary strain,
Her desperate men attain
Her rigging, there to gain
    What seems but slower death.

But hope now thrills their breast,
For o'er the billows' crest

The life-boat speeds, attest
    Of selfless souls that dare ;
And every man finds place
Within her crowded space
Save one, whose helpless case
    Seems all beyond their care.

Then Harro ran to meet
The boat with flying feet,
And cried, with joy complete,
    "All ? All ? Ye have saved all ?"—
"All, Captain, all but one,
And he so high had run
Upon the mast, that none
    Was equal to the call."

At this he smote his head,
And with sad sternness said,
"'Tis woe that those I've led
    Should fail in duty's hest ! . . .
Now let but four agree
To try yon wreck with me,
And that lone wretch shall be
    With life divinely blest."

"Comrade, In vain thy plea,
Too heavy runs the sea."
"Then I alone," said he,
 Will venture on the deed."
"Not so," upstarted four,
"If thou but lead, once more
We'll through these billows bore,
 Despite all coward rede."

"Harro, my only boy,
Do not all hope and joy
Within my breast destroy,"
 His tearful mother cried;
"The sea runs higher still,
And great as is thy skill,
And stout thy strength and will,
 It cannot be defied.

"Our duty's charge by none
More nobly has been done;
And as for that poor one
 So lonely left, he's gone;
'Tis sure we cannot know
That he still lives, and so

129

The truest might forego
              What thy fond wish is on.

"Thou'rt all that's left to me:
Thy brother Uwe, he
Went from me, and the sea
        Most like has been his grave;
And thy dear sire doth sleep
Entombed within the deep,
Where hope had bade him reap
        The glory of the brave.

"I cannot let thee go;
The ocean is our foe,
And these mad breakers throw
        Fresh terror on the strand."
"But what of him out there,
Abandoned to despair?
Has *he* no mother's care?"
        Asked Harro oar in hand.

Again she pleading cried:
"Give o'er thy spirit's pride,
Come to my lonely side,
        Nor perish in the storm."

In vain ;—the four and he,
With sturdy arm and free,
Sent through the seething sea
    The life-boat's glorious form.

They conquered wave and blast,
And safely clutched at last
The mast where still clung fast
    The wretch about to die ;
When Harro then straightway
Clomb, without pause or stay,
To where that lone one lay
    All stark against the sky.

With more than tender care
His burden he did bear
Unto his comrades there,
    Who clove the air with cheers ;
But when they saw the face
Upturned to his embrace,
Another joy did lace
    Their cheeks with silent tears.

Homeward, with heartening song,
They drove the boat along,

Mid joys that there did throng

From perils all had braved;

And when they neared the shore,

'Twas Harro shouted o'er:

"Good mother, grieve no more,

'Tis Uwe we have saved."

INVOCATION TO SAN FRANCISCO

READ AT THE UNITARIAN CLUB DINNER ON MARCH 29, 1898,
AT WHICH WAS DISCUSSED "MUNICIPAL PROBLEMS."

O City of our life and hope,

That sittest by this westmost sea,

Thy lovers pray thy widest scope,

And deepest in the yet to be.

May Learning's temples rear their towers

Above thy unpolluted ways,

And all the strength of all thy powers

Build only what good men can praise.

May stranger ships bring costly bales

From every near and distant land,

And in return thy wingèd sails

By prosperous winds he ever fanned.

May all the arts with newer life,

And greater, sing their highest notes;

While over all with glory rife

The flag of peace divinely floats.

O City of our life and hope,

That sittest by this westmost sea,

So long as we have strength to cope,

God lead that strength to truth and thee.

MY FRIEND

He had completeness: Gentleman and Man
Bloomed in his nature a compósite flower;
The grace and elegance of mien that can
Alone assure us that the subtile power
Of pure refinement every action rules,
High culture, dignity and gentleness,
All these were his. And in the sterner schools,
Where none but souls that vigorously press
Forever onward win the world's success,
He was as sturdy as a man might be.
And with it all, pretentious ne'er was he,
But went his way with charming modesty.

133

In Memoriam

My dear, departed boy, these songs I lay
Upon the urn that holds thy hallowed clay;
Wrung from the fibres of my heart they are —
That heart which wears immedicable scar.

But six and twenty years on earth he knew;
  And from the time his eyes first saw the day,
  Until death blinded them forever, they
  Cast but affection's glances from their blue.
And in their light such confidences grew
  And genial joys, that home became the stay
  That held him fast when he was far away
  And once more drew him to his cherished few.
Machinery was his goddess at whose shrine
  With nimble fingers and inventive brain
  He poured unstintedly his life's best wine.
So young, so good, to die! That sad refrain,
  Wet with his dear ones' tears that blend with
     mine,
  Makes heavier my intolerable pain.

AMONG THE WHEELS

TO P. T. T.

With heavy heart I went amid the hum
　Of whirring wheels that owe their life to thee,
　And where thou hadst full often greeted me
　With love that made it more than joy to come;
But all their music was to me as dumb
　As if thy hand had never set it free:
　For thy dear, welcoming face I could not see,
　And Grief but added to her bitter sum.
Then Peace drew near me and upon my head
　Most softly laid her spirit-soothing palm,
　As with the gentlest tenderness she said:
Remember, after storm there must be calm;
　And know, these wheels now sing rejoicing psalm
　For him who lives in them though he be dead.

DREAMS

I know not why so wearisome to me
  My necessary tasks appear to-day,
  Save that my brood of dreams is fain to play
 ˌWhere all things beautiful are wont to be.
This very moment do I feel so free
  That nought could hold me under tasking sway,
  As borne beyond the city's strenuous way
  I float in soundless, calm serenity.
And now the mountains woo me on and on,
  And many a lake lays bare her crystal breast,
  While scene on scene its pillared beauty rears.
O dreams that mock! for from me HE has gone
  Who shared these joys with me; and grief-oppressed
  I sink to earth o'erweighted with my tears.

TO P. T. T.

The strangest thing that ever came to me,
  Since first my being conscious feeling knew,
  Was that relentless pain which pierced me through
  When Death unmerciful had power o'er thee:
That thou nowhere in all this world canst be,
  Thy voice forever mute that rang so true,
  Oh, who can sound the depths of such adieu
  Till made acquainted with its agony?
But when I saw thee in thy coffin laid,
  A rare, new beauty shone upon thy face
  So gracious and so wonderful to see,
That Death's own self I could not then upbraid,
  For through my tears my vision seemed to trace
  Thy flight to higher than mortality.

DIRGE

In these sad days when Joy outspreads her wing
    Grief's unrestrained pursuers to elude,
    Sudden she feels the shaft, and thence subdued
    Falls down to earth a wounded, anguished thing.
Then Grief from out her loneliest cave doth bring
    Upon the scene her melancholy brood,
    And bids no note of happiness intrude
    As these alone in dirge's numbers sing:
Oh, mourn for him who in his promise died;
    For him who held his course by Duty's pole;
    For him whose cup of love was filled to brim.
Remember how he stood when he was tried,
    Remember those great hopes that stirred his soul,
    Remember all he was, and mourn for him.

I would not have the world's regardless eyes
   Rest on this verse made consecrate with tears
   For him who in the blossom of his years
   Sank down o'erburdened, nevermore to rise;
But those alone whose unavailing cries
   Have risen like mine for all the heart endears
   I would have here to pause, and in his bier's
   Deep shadow share my bosom's agonies.
Yet as Grief hands the bitter cup around,
   And deeper grows the shade's intensity,
   My soul may hear some new, far-falling sound;
And midst its throbs divine it then may be
   That Life will stream with richer thought on me,
   And Death seem monarch with effulgence crowned.

TO DEATH

Thou monster Death, that dost no mercy show
  To least or greatest of the earthly train;
  That hast made horrible thine endless reign
  With tear-cemented monuments of woe!
Thou angel Death, that kindly dost bestow
  Release from hopeless ill, from torturing pain,
  And from life's whirling flood where fiercely strain
  The desperate souls that faint and sink below!
Like Love thou art as old as oldest eld,
  Yet ever new as is the wondrous child
  This moment blossomed on its mother's breast;
And since the time that thou wast first beheld,
  When Order's music rang through Chaos wild,
  Life has by thee been nourished and caressed.

ENVOY

Thy work is done, and what thou hadst to do
  Was wrought with faithfulness and all thy might,
  Nor darker made is now my sorrow's night
  By thought that thou wast ever less than true.
What flowers more sweet than these could Love
    bestrew
  On tomb of any man though Son of Light
  With dazzling fame immaculately white,
  Or conquering one whose sword its millions slew?
Thy mortal ashes rest within the urn;
  Thy fleshly substance is dissolved in air
  Or throbs with newer life in many a cell;
Thy spirit is a star whose light will burn,
  We trust, so deeply and divinely fair,
  That Grief herself shall feel that all is well.

Translations

Why heed the critics who delight to dart
Their sneer-tipped arrows at translator's art?
The poet's work remains his own at last
Though it in other languages be cast,
And in the sky of Fame it still will shine
By that which made it at the first divine.
But in this foreign dress some soul may see
A hint of that which fascinated me;
Some deep impression be still deeper made
When by our muse-belovèd tongue conveyed;
Some beauty be with newer beauty set;
Some thought that will with fresh emotion fret
Some gentle breast, or with strange music sweep
O'er heaving waters of the spirit's deep.

FROM A WINNOWER OF GRAIN TO
THE WINDS

(AFTER JOACHIM DU BELLAY)

Nimble troop, to you

>That on light pinion through

>The world forever pass,

>And with a murmuring sweet

>Where shade and verdure meet

>Toss gently leaf and grass,

I give these violets,

>Lilies and flowerets,

>And roses here that blow,

>All these red-blushing roses

>Whose freshness now uncloses,

>And these rich pinks also.

With your soft breath now deign

>To fan the spreading plain,

>And fan, too, this retreat,

>Whilst I with toil and strain

>Winnow my golden grain

>In the day's scorching heat.

FROM THE MISCELLANEOUS POEMS OF
VOLTAIRE:

TO A LADY
ON SENDING HER A RING ON WHICH WAS
ENGRAVED THE AUTHOR'S PORTRAIT

These features Barier graved for you alone:
O deign to find them fit for you to see:
Yours in my heart were better cut, and own
A master greater far than he.

––––––––

TO MADAME DU CHATELET
ON RECEIVING HER PORTRAIT

O living image, features dear,
Of that fond object of my passion's smart!
Yet that which love has graved upon my heart
Than this is thousand times more near.

TO A PRATER

In writing, thought should lead the way: *From*
Better erase the senseless blot. *Voltaire*

Authors at times write on without a thought,
As some speak oft without a word to say.

EPIGRAM

ON THE DEATH OF MONSIEUR D'AUBE, NEPHEW OF MONSIEUR DE FONTENELLE

Who is it knocks? said Lucifer.— *From*
Open, 'tis d'Aube. At this name's stir, *Voltaire*
All helldom fled and left him lone.
Oh, oh! said d'Aube, this land, I see,
Treats me as Paris treated me:
Whene'er I made a call, I found not anyone.

EPIGRAM

From Voltaire Know you that noteless poetaster who,
Dust-dry and stiff, is cold and hard all through;
Having the slanderer's bite without his art,
Who ne'er can please much less can wound the heart;
Who for misdeeds in prison walls did fare,
And afterwards was flogged at Saint-Lazare,
Chased, beaten and detested for his crimes,
Disgraced, despised, derided for his rhymes;
And who, contented in a cuckold's sty,
Chatters about himself unceasingly?
Eh! 'tis the poet Roy, at once all cry.

FAREWELL TO LIFE

AT PARIS, 1778.

Farewell !—the country I go to
Still holds my late dear father yet;
My friends, farewell fore'er to you
Who may for me bear some regret.
Laugh, enemies, for so to do
Will pay the usual requiem debt.
Still, some day you may feel concern:
For when to darksome shores consigned,
Your works you there would seek to find,
On you the laugh will have its turn.

    When on the stage of human life
A man can play his part no more,
On leaving, all the air is rife
With hisses to his exit door.
I've seen in their last malady
Full many a one of differing states:
Old bishops, agèd magistrates,
Old courtesans, in agony.
In vain, all ceremoniously,
Together with its little bell

*From
Voltaire*

Farewell to Life Came sacred gear of sacristy;

Vainly the priest anointed well

Our friend in his extremity;

The public laughed with malice fell;

A moment satire joyed to dwell

On all his life's absurdity;

Then even his name no one could tell—

The farce had reached finality.

And now my utmost bound I own,

What man needs less compassion's tear?

'Tis he alone knows nought of fear,

Who lives and dies to fame unknown.

THE TOMB AND THE ROSE

(FROM "LES VOIX INTÉRIEURES" OF VICTOR HUGO)

The Tomb said to the Rose: "Love's own,
What mak'st thou of the tears bestrown
By lovely, dewy dawn o'er thee?"
The Rose said to the Tomb: "And pray,
What comes of that which feeds alway
Thy gulf that yawns eternally?"

Then said the Rose: "O sombre Tomb,
I make of them a rare perfume
Where honey with the amber lies."
Then said the Tomb: "O plaintive Flower,
Of every soul that feels my power
I make an angel of the skies!"

COME NEAR ME WHEN I SLEEP

(FROM " LES RAYONS ET LES OMBRES " OF VICTOR HUGO)

Oh, when I sleep, come closely to my couch
As did fair Laura to Petrarca's side,
And as I feel thy breathing's balmy touch . . .—
      Sudden my lips
      Will part to thine.

When on my brow, where then perchance some dream
Of darkness settles which too long would bide,
Thy lovely eyes look down with starry beam . . .—
      Sudden my dream
      Will brightly shine.

Then if my lips, whose fluttering flame has learned
Love's lightning God himself has purified,
Are kissed by thee—to woman angel turned . . .—
      Sudden will wake
      This soul of mine.

IN THE CEMETERY OF . . . .

(FROM "LES RAYONS ET LES OMBRES" OF VICTOR HUGO)

The laughing living crowd by folly still is led,
At times where pleasure rules, at times where anguish
      lies,
But here these all forgotten, silent, lonely dead
On me, a dreamer, fix their sad, regardful eyes.

They know me to be man of solitary mood,
A musing, strolling one who on the trees attends,
The soul that sadly learns, from sorrow's countless
      brood,
In trouble all begins, in peace all trouble ends !

They well do know the pensive, reverent mien of mine
Mid crosses, graves and boxwood, and they mutely list
To fallen leaves that 'neath my careless foot repine,
And they have seen me dream in woods the shades
      have kissed.

O blatant living ones of strife and mad unrest,
My flowing voice falls better on these dead ones' ears !
My lyre's sweet hymns that lie deep hidden in my breast
That are but songs for you, for them are gushing tears.

Forgotten by the living, nature still is theirs:
In garden of the dead where each shall end his dreams,
In more celestial garb, and calmer, dawn appears,
Still lovelier is bird, and lily purer seems.

'Tis there I live!—there pluck the rose of pallid face,
Console with tombs that lie in desolation rent;
I pass, repass, the branches gently there displace,
And stir the sighing grass; the dead they are content.

'Tis there I dream; and roaming many a drowseful
　　　space,
With thought-enwidened eyes I marvellously see
My soul transformed as in a magic-haunted place,
Mysterious mirror of the vast immensity.

The wandering beetles there I indolently watch,
The wavering branches, forms, and color-glinting gleams,
And on the fallen stones reposing love to catch
The dazzlings of the flowers and of the myriad beams.

'Tis dream's ideal fills my wondering eyesight there,
Floating in shining veil between the earth and me;
And there my ingrate doubts are melted into prayer:
For standing I begin and end upon my knee.

As in the rock, whose hollow drips in sunless gloom,
For drop of water seeks the thirsty, humble dove,
So now my altered spirit seeks the shadeful tomb,
To drink, if but a sip, of faith, of hope and love.

WHAT IS HEARD ON THE MOUNTAIN

(FROM "LES FEUILLES D'AUTOMNE" OF VICTOR HUGO)

Has it so been that you in calmful, silent wise,
Have pushed to mountain's top in presence of the skies?
Was this on banks of Sund? on shores of Brittany?
And at the mountain's foot did you the ocean see?
And leaned o'er surging wave, and o'er immensity,
In silent wise and calmful, have you bent your ear?
'Tis this befalls : at least, one day at dream's command
My thought had drooped in flight above a shimmering
       strand,
And, to the briny depths plunging from summit sheer,
On one hand saw the sea, on the other saw the land ;
And listening there I heard a voice whose parallel
Ne'er issued from a mouth and on an ear ne'er fell.

At first its sound was full, confused, all unconfined,

More vague than in the tufted trees the sighing wind;

With piercing concords filled, with murmurs suavely
low;

Sweet as an evening song, as harsh as armors' shock

When fight's red furies round the maddened squadrons
flock,

And in the clarion's mouths with battle's fierceness
blow.

'Twas music past all thought, with notes divinely deep,

Which, fluid, round the world unceasingly did sweep,

And in the boundless heavens, its waves fore'er renewed,

Rolled, in its orbit's greatening, endless vastitude,

To lowest depths profound, until its flow sublime

Was lost in dark with Number, Form, and Space, and
Time!

As with another air, dispersed, outreaching wide,

The globe's whole body felt the hymn's eternal tide;

And as the world is wafted in its airy sea,

So now 'twas wafted in this mighty symphony.

Then the ethereal harps swept o'er my pensive soul,

Lost in their voice as in great ocean's surging roll.

And soon I then discerned, clouded and dissonant,

Two voices in this voice each with the other blent,

O'erflowing all the earth to very firmament,

That hymned together there the universal chant;

And in their roar profound mine ear caught every stave,

As one two currents sees which cross beneath the wave.

One came the waters o'er: blest hymn! a glory-song!

It was the voice of waves that spoke in happy throng;

The other from the land that rose where now we are

Was sad; it was men's murmur rising near and far;

And in this diapason, which day and night sang on,

Each billow had its voice, each man his separate tone.

But, as I've said, the Ocean, vast, magnificent,

A mild and joyous voice through endless spaces sent;

Like harp in Zion's fanes it burst in swelling note,

And with creation's praise song filled its raptured throat.

His music, borne by zephyrs as by gales that fly,

Incessantly toward God in triumph mounted high,

And when each throbbing wave, that God alone can
    quell,

Had quired in joy another rose in songful swell.

Like that great lion of whom brave Daniel was the guest,

159

At times the Ocean's voice dropped low within his
    breast,
And then I deemed I saw toward the fiery West
Upon his mane of gold the hand of God impressed.

Yet, nathless, by the side of this so great fanfare
The other voice,—like cry of steed in maddening scare,
Like rusted hinge of gate that guards Hell's quenchless
    fire,
Like brazen bow drawn o'er the strings of iron lyre,—
Ground harsh ; and insult, tears, anathema, and cries,
Viaticum, baptism, refused by him who dies,
The blasphemy and curse and rage from mouths that
    rave,
In human clamor's whirling, all-devouring wave,
Passed by, as in the vale where shuddering shadows
    cling
Do Night's ill-omened birds with dusky, hideous wing.
What was that sound which made a thousand echoes
    rise ?
Alas ! it was the earth and man all torn with cries.

Brothers, of these two voices, the strangest ever sped,
That cease not though reborn, and cease not being fled,

That shake the eternal ear with everlasting stroke,
HUMANITY in one, in the other, NATURE spoke.

Thought brooded o'er me, for my faithful spirit then
Alas ! had never yet attained to such high ken,
Nor had such lustrous light illumed my shadeful day;
And I considered long, turning at times away
From that obscure abyss the billows hid from me
To the other gulf that filled my own immensity.
And then I asked myself, why is it we are here,
What is this life and what its agony and tear,
And what the soul, and why should any being be ?
Why should the Lord, who reads alone his book, decree
Eternally to blend in hymen's fatal tie
The song of nature with the human race's cry ?

THE PELICAN

(FROM ALFRED DE MUSSET'S "LA NUIT DE MAI")

When wearied pelican returns from lengthened quest
Unto his lonely reeds where evening mists hang low,
His famished little ones all shoreward wildly go
On seeing him afar alight on billow's crest.
And then believing spoil is theirs to seize and share,
With joyous cries they to their father quickly fare,
As o'er their hideous goitres shake their ravening beaks.
With dragging step and slow he gains a towering rock,
Where shielding with his pendent wings his starving flock
He, melancholy fisher, all the sky bespeaks.
From out his open breast the blood makes copious way,
For vainly sought he ocean's depths on eager wings;
They empty were and even the strand was stripped of prey;
And now for nourishment his heart alone he brings.
Sombre and silent, stretched upon the lonely stone,
The father shares his deepest with the sons his own;
And in this love sublime he rocks his dolor till,
As he views flowing fast the crimson of his breast
And sinks and staggers by this feast of death possessed,
Joy, tenderness and horror all his senses thrill.

But mid this sacrifice divine at moments he
Is sickened with the thought of too long agony,
For now he sees his children will but give him death.
Then rising up he opes his wings to ocean's breath,
And striking hard his heart with madly savage cry,
Along the night his woeful farewell notes so roll
That all the sea-birds from the shore in terror fly,
And traveller there belated, feeling death is nigh,
With dread's appalling fears commends to God his soul.

THE POET

(FROM ALFRED DE MUSSET'S "LA NUIT DE MAI")

O Muse! thou most insatiate sprite,
Do not demand so much of me.
Man nothing on the sand doth write
When blows the north-wind bitterly.
Time was my youthful lips were stirred
And ever ready as a bird
With ceaseless song the hours to speed;
But I have borne such pangs of fire,
That were the least that I desire
Essayed by me upon my lyre,
It then would break it as a reed.

163

IMPROMPTU
IN RESPONSE TO THE QUESTION:
WHAT IS POETRY?

(AFTER ALFRED DE MUSSET)

To drive the chase in every hallowed spot
By Memory haunted, and the captured thought,
All tremulous, uncertain, firm to hold
Balanced on axis glorious of gold ;
To stamp eternity upon the dream
Which but an instant lights him with its gleam;
Deeply to love the beautiful and true,
And their harmonious virtues to pursue ;
In his own heart to look and list unto
The echo of his genius ; all alone
To sing, to laugh, and make his tearful moan,
Thereto unprompted by design or guile ;
Out of a sigh, a word, a look, and even a smile,
A work of art consummately to rear
Full of sweet charmingness and moving fear ;
A radiant pearl to fashion from a tear:
Such is the passion of the poet's strife,
His boon, his great ambition, and his life.

SONG

(AFTER ALFRED DE MUSSET)

Good morn, Suzon, my woodland flower!
    Art still the prettiest thing to see?
I have returned, as thou must know,
    From wondrous trip to Italy!
Of Paradise I've made the round—
Have written verse—in love been bound . . .
        What's that to thee!
        What's that to thee!
Before thee comes thy waiting one:
        Ope thy door!
        Ope thy door!
            Good morn, Suzon!

I saw thee in the lilacs' time,
    When thy free heart was in its bud,
And thou did'st say: "I've no desire
    For love as yet to stir my blood."
Since then, what, pray, has been thy fate?
Who leaves too soon returns too late.
        What's that to me?
        What's that to me?

Song   Before thee comes thy waiting one:

Ope thy door!

Ope thy door!

Good morn, Suzon!

ADIEU, SUZON!
SONG
(AFTER ALFRED DE MUSSET)

Adieu, Suzon, my sweet, blonde rose,
Who for a week has made me blest:
Of all the world's supreme delights,
The short amour is oft the best.
Ah, whither shall my errant star,
On leaving thee, tempt me to stray?
Yet I must go, my little one,
With hastening pace, and far away,
     Still ever on.

I leave thee; on mine eager lip
Burns once again thy parting kiss;
Within mine arms, imprudent dear,

Thy beauteous head finds soothing bliss.

Feel'st thou my heart's delirious beat?

How thine doth make responsive play!

Yet I must go, my little one,

With hastening pace, and far away,

      Fore'er thine own.

Paf! that's my horse they're saddling now;—

When on the road, how then withstand

The perfume of thy baleful hair,

That has so scented all my hand!

Thou hypocrite, I see thee smile

While running off in nymph-like play.

Yet I must go, my little one,

With hastening pace, and far away,

      Still laughing on.

Oh, all of sadness and of charm,

Dear child, is in thy fond adieu!

'Tis maddening joy to see thy heart

Shine in thine eyes thy tear-drops through.

In life, thy trancing look allures;

In death, 'twill be my latest stay.

Yet I must go, my little one,

With hastening pace, and far away,
        Lamenting on.

Oh, that our love, shouldst thou forget,
Might for one moment be revived
Like some bouquet of drooping flowers
Within thy charming bosom hived !
Adieu : good fortune stays at home ;
But memory shall not say me nay :
And that I'll take, my little one,
With hastening pace, and far away,
        'Neath every sun.

MARY STUART'S FAREWELL

(AFTER BÉRANGER)

Farewell, delightful land of France,
    Where all my love doth lie ;
Home of my childhood's gay romance,
Farewell ! to leave thee is to die.

O thou adopted country mine,
That seest me banished from thy shore,
List to thy Mary's sad farewell,
And guard her memory evermore.

The wind is up, we quit the strand,
And all my tears and sobs are vain;
God will not stir the angry waves,
To beat me back to thee again.

Farewell, delightful land of France,
    Where all my love doth lie;
Home of my childhood's gay romance,
Farewell! to leave thee is to die.

When thy loved people saw me wreathed
With thy resplendent fleur-de-lis,
My charms in all their springtime bloom
Won plaudits rank could ne'er decree.
Ah, vain the royal pomp and state
The gloomy Scot intends for me;
I would not wish to be a queen,
Unless to reign, as once, o'er thee.

Farewell, delightful land of France,
    Where all my love doth lie;
Home of my childhood's gay romance,
Farewell! to leave thee is to die.

Love, glory, genius, these have filled
With too much joy my beauteous days;

169

Mary Stuart's Farewell

In Scotia's rough, uncultured land
My fate will find far different ways.
Alas! already, big with doom,
An omen bids my heart stand still;
For I have seen, in dreadful dream,
A scaffold raised my blood to spill.

Farewell, delightful land of France,
    Where all my love doth lie;
Home of my childhood's gay romance,
Farewell! to leave thee is to die.

Dear France, in midst of all her fears
The daughter of the Stuart line,
As on this day which sees her tears,
Will turn toward thee as to a shrine.
But, God! the ship with rapid keel
Already bends 'neath foreign skies,
And night draws down her dewy veil,
To screen thee from my weeping eyes.

Farewell! delightful land of France,
    Where all my love doth lie;
Home of my childhood's gay romance,
Farewell! to leave thee is to die.

FIFTY YEARS

(AFTER BÉRANGER)

What mean these flowers? Is it my fête?
No; this bouquet now comes to say,
That half a century on my head
Is rounded and complete to-day.
How many days fleet fast along!
How many moments fruitless pass!
How many wrinkles tell their tale!
I'm fifty years. Alas! Alas!

At such an age we nothing hold;
The fruit dies on the sallowing tree—
But some one knocks;—yet open not:
My part is ended, that I see.
I'll wage some doctor thrusts his card,
Or 'tis the *Times*; ah, day there was,
I would have said: That is Lisette.
I'm fifty years. Alas! Alas!

Old age is cursed with biting ills:
The gout is murder's willing tool;
Blindness for us welds prison chains;

While at our deafness mocks the fool.

Then reason, like expiring lamp,

Burns faint and trembling ere it pass.

O children, honor hoary age.

I'm fifty years.   Alas!   Alas!

Heavens! Here's Death ;—rubbing his hands

With joyous glee, he comes apace.

'Tis gravedigger that's at my door ;

Farewell, good sirs of every race !

Below, are famine, pest and war ;

Above, the stars' resplendent mass.

Open, while God remains to me.

I'm fifty years.   Alas!   Alas!

But no ;—'tis you ! my welcome friend,

Sister of Charity of loves !

You draw my sleeping soul from out

The horrid thoughts wherein it moves ;

Strewing the roses of your youth,

As does the Spring, where'er you pass,

And sweetening all an old man's dreams.

I'm fifty years.   Alas!   Alas!

JACQUES

(AFTER BÉRANGER)

Dear Jacques, I must bid thee awake :
A bailiff scours the village round,
With keeper following at his heels.
Poor man, they come the tax to take.

Get up, my Jacques, get up :
Here comes the bailiff of the King.

Look out and see : the night is gone ;
Never before hast slept so late ;
Thou know'st to sell to old Remi,
That one must stir before the dawn.

Get up, my Jacques, get up :
Here comes the bailiff of the King.

We've not a sou ! O God of fate !
I hear him ; how the dogs do bark ;
He will demand a whole month's pay.
Ah, if the King could only wait !

Jacques   Get up, my Jacques, get up:
Here comes the bailiff of the King.

Oh, how the poor are stripped and flayed!
So crushed are we, we own all told,
For us, thy father and six boys,
Nought but my distaff and thy spade.

Get up, my Jacques, get up:
Here comes the bailiff of the King.

They count that with our wretched hut
An acre's fourth is far too much;
Yet that with hopeless misery reeks,
While this by usury's scythe is cut.

Get up, my Jacques, get up:
Here comes the bailiff of the King.

So much of pain, of gains so few.
When shall we taste pork flesh again?
Ah, strengthening food is all so dear!
And even the salt, and sugar, too!

Get up, my Jacques, get up:
Here comes the bailiff of the King.

Some wine to thee would courage bring; Jacques
But then the laws are close and hard;
My dearest, for some drink for thee
Go sell at once my wedding ring.

Get up, my Jacques, get up:
Here comes the bailiff of the King.

Couldst dream that thy good angel would
To thee bring plenty and repose?
Dost think taxation bites the rich?
Their barns to all the rats give food.

Get up, my Jacques, get up:
Here comes the bailiff of the King.

He enters! Heavens! O woe of woes!
Thou speak'st no word! Thou art so pale!
On yesterday thou mad'st some wail,
From whom before no murmur rose.

Get up, my Jacques, get up:
Here's the good bailiff of the King.

Jacques Her cries are vain: there is no life.

For him who wears toil's thorny crown

Death is a pillow soft as down.

Good people, pray ye for his wife.

Get up, my Jacques, get up:

Here's the good bailiff of the King.

THE VASE

(AFTER LECONTE DE LISLE)

Take, shepherd of the goat and of the frugal ewe,

This two-eared vase, well-waxed, and from the chisel
> new.

Its wood still fragrant smells, and round its edge enwind

The ivy's verdurous leaves with helichrysum twined

And clustering fruits of gold. Ah, firm the hand and
> fine

That here did carve this form of woman so divine;

With peplum graced and brow enwreathed with flowers
> she smiles

At her contending suitors with their fruitless wiles.

Upon the rock, his feet in tangled wrack where he *The Vase*
Now drags his long net toward the smooth and glaucous
      sea,
A fisher comes apace; and though with age bent o'er,
His rigid muscles swell as strains he more and more.
Near by a laden vine with ripened grapes bends low,
'Neath which a young boy sits to guard it from the foe;
But two sly foxes steal upon the other side,
And eat the grapes as they behind the branches hide,
The while the child inweaves, from fragile straws
      with care,
And from some blades of rush, a deft cicala-snare;
While all around the vase and Dorian plinth thou'lt see
The acanthus leaf displayed in beauty's luxury.

This masterpiece has cost me pains and money too—
A cheese both large and fresh, and fine, young pregnant
      ewe.
Shepherd, 'tis thine whose songs are sweeter far to me
Than figs of Ægilus, and wake Pan's jealousy.

SOLAR HERCULES

(AFTER LECONTE DE LISLE)

O pang-born Tamer who as swaddled infant killed

The Night's fell Dragons! O thou Warrior, Lion-
     Heart,

Who pierced bane-breathing Hydra with thy burning
     dart

Where poisonous mist and mire their livid horrors
     spilled ;

And who with flawless sight of old saw Centaurs start

At precipices' verge and wheel with rearing breast !

Of all the genial Gods, the eldest, fairest, best !

O purifier King, who through thy glorious days,

Made, as so many torches, from the East to West,

The sacrificial fire on every summit blaze !

Thy golden quiver's void, the Shade's at last thy goal.

Hail Glory of the Air ! All vainly thou dost tear,

With thy convulsive hands where flames in rivers roll,

The bloody clouds which wreathe thy pyre divine,
     and there

In purple whirlwind now thou yieldest up thy soul !

THE CONDOR'S SLEEP

(AFTER LECONTE DE LISLE)

Beyond the Cordilleras' stairs that steeply wind,
Beyond black eagle's haunts in mist-enshrouded air,
And higher than the cratered, furrowed summits where
The boiling flood of lava rages unconfined,
His pendent pinions tinct with spots of crimson dye,
The great bird silent views, with indolent, dull stare,
America and space outreaching boundless there,
And that now sombre sun which dies in his cold eye.
Night rolls from out the East, where savage pampas lie
Beneath the tier on tier of peaks in endless line;
It Chili lulls, the shores, the cities' roar and cry,
The grand Pacific Sea, and horizon all divine;
The silent continent its close embraces hide:
On sands and hills, in gorges, on declivities,
And on the heights, now swell, in widening vortices,
The heavy flood and flow of its high-rolling tide.
Upon a lofty peak, alone, like spectre grim,
Bathed in a light that spills its life-blood on the snow,
He waits this direful sea that threats him as a foe:
It comes, it breaks in foam, and dashes over him.

In the unfathomed depths the Southern Cross doth loom
Upon the sky's vast shore a pharos-shining light.
His rattling throat speaks joy, he proudly shakes his
plume,
His muscular, peeled neck he lifts and stretches tight ;
To raise himself he gives the hard snow lashing stings ;
Then with a raucous cry he mounts where no winds are,
And from the dark globe far, far from the living star,
In the icy air he sleeps on grand, outspreading wings.

TO A DEAD POET

(AFTER LECONTE DE LISLE)

Thou whose delighted eye roamed eagerly and free
From hues divine to forms in strength immortal grown,
And from the fleshly to the heavens' star-splendored zone,
In that dark night which seals thy lids peace be to thee.

To see, to hear, to feel? Breath, dust and vanity.
To love? That golden cup has but the bitter known.
Thou'rt like some wearied God who leaves his altars
        lone,
To mingled be with matter's vast immensity.

Upon thy mute grave where thy mouldering body lies
Whether or no the tears are poured from sorrowing eyes,
Whether thy banal age forget thee or acclaim,

I envy thee thy silent, darksome bed below,
Forever freed from life and never more to know
Man's horror of his own existence and the shame.

MY SECRET

(AFTER FELIX ARVERS)

My soul its secret has, my life its mystery :
'Tis an eternal love an instant saw conceived.
My pain's beyond all hope, so silent I must be,
While she, the cause, knows not that I am sore bereaved.

Alas ! I shall have passed anear her unperceived,
Still by her side, and yet a lonely one to see,
And shall have served on earth to life's extremity,
Not daring aught to ask, and having nought received.

Though God has made her sweet and infinitely dear,
With heedless mind she'll go her way, and never hear
The murmuring of love that doth her steps attend.

Beneath the pious yoke of duty's rigid sway,
When she reads o'er this verse all full of her, she'll say,
" This woman, who is she ? " and will not comprehend.

THE LADY'S ANSWER

(AFTER LOUIS AIGOIN)

My friend, wherefore aver, with so much mystery,
That the eternal love within your breast conceived
Is pain beyond all hope, a secret that must be ;
And why suppose that she may know not you're bereaved?

Ah no, you did not pass anear her unperceived,
Nor should you've deemed yourself a lonely one to see ;
The best beloved may serve to life's extremity,
Not daring aught to ask, and having nought received.

The good God gives to us a knowing heart and dear,
And on our way we find that it is sweet to hear
The murmuring of love that doth our steps attend.

She who would meekly bow to duty's rigid sway,
Reading your verse of her, felt more than she can say :
For though she spake no word, . . . she well did
    comprehend.

183

PHILOSOPHY

(AFTER TAINE)

Two sages well have known the verity supreme ;
But wrongly each the other condemns and says him nay ;
One tells us : " Bear thou up, be strong and patient
      aye " ;
The other : " Happy be, enjoy each moment's dream."

Zeno and Epicurus, on the antique trireme,
To either shore have pressed too closely on their way;
While we, in seeking port, have stranded even as they.
And yet the cats have solved the problem's knotty
      scheme :

The pleasure as it comes, the pain that will not fly,
You, Puss, accept unquestioned ; and the sun on high,
When in the boundless blue at eve he journeys hence,

Sees you, in circle couched, as at morn's earliest call,
Without an effort happy, and resigned to all,
Serenely smooth your tail in calm indifference.

MY BOHEMIA

A FANTASY

(AFTER ARTHUR RIMBAUD)

With fists in tattered pockets forth I strayed,—
My great-coat, too, not far from raggery,—
Beneath the skies, O Muse, most true to thee ;
And there what radiant love-dreams round me played !
My only breeches gaped with holes as I,
Poor, little dreamer, many a rhyme dropped where
My footsteps fared ; mine inn the heavens' Great Bear,
'Neath stars whose soft, sweet rustlings filled the sky.

I heard them as I sat by roadsides when
September's eves were steeped in balm ; and then,
As with strong wine, my face was wet with dew ;
And rhyming midst fantastic shades I made
Of my torn shoe's elastics, worn and frayed,
A lyre as near my heart my foot I drew.

NOTE.—Mr. Lloyd Mifflin calls my attention to the original of this sonnet
and to the fact that Mr. George Moore, in his "Impressions and Opinions,"
says that Rimbaud wrote it at the age of fifteen years, and that it was never
before published until it was published in his (Moore's) volume with title as
above

THE VIOLET

(AFTER GOETHE)

Unknown a violet bowed its head
Where meadow in its beauty spread—
A violet fresh and lovely,
As youthful shepherdess came there,
And with light step and winsome air
Along, along,
The meadow went and sang.

"Ah!" thought the violet, "would that I
Were grandest flower beneath the sky,
Instead of violet lowly,
By her dear hand to be uptorn
And on her gracious bosom worn,
If but, if but,
A little quarter-hour."

But ah! on it the maiden bent
No glance at all, but as she went
The violet poor she trampled.
Yet still it sank in joyful state:
"I die, indeed, but glorious fate,
Through her, through her,
And at her very feet."

THE ANGLER

(AFTER GOETHE)

The water rushed in swelling flow;
    An Angler plied his art
As sat he filled with calm, and cool
    Up to the very heart;
And as he lurked with slyness there,
    And motionless did spy,
Amazed he saw the tide upheave,
    Divide itself on high,
And from the cleft a Naiad rise
    Before his dazzled eye.

She sang to him; she spake to him:
    "My brood why dost thou snare,
With human wit and human craft,
    To scorching death of air?
Ah, friend of mine! if thou wouldst know
    What joys my children share
Upon the ground where they disport,
    Unknown to ills or care,
Thou shouldst descend and be at once
    Rejuvenated there.

187

The
Angler   "Do not the Sun and Moon repose
         Refreshed on Ocean's breast?
Turn not their welcome faces there
         Upon us doubly blest,
As from the sparkling wave they rise
         With newer life imprest?
Allure thee not the Heavens deep,
         The humid, glorious Blue?
Decoys thee not thy mirrored form
         Down to perpetual dew?"

The water rushed in swelling flow;
         It laved his naked feet;
His heart unconsciously grew full
         Of fond desire's heat,
As if his own beloved had come
         His offered kiss to meet.
She spake to him; she sang to him;
         No hand could intervene:
She drew him half, half sank he down
         And nevermore was seen.

UNDER THE LINDEN

(FROM GOETHE'S FAUST)

All for the dance the shepherd dressed;
In ribbon, wreath and coloured vest,
 Sprucely himself arraying;
Beneath the Linden's green expanse
The crowd began like mad to dance;
  Huzza! Huzza!
  Hey-day-héy! Hey! Hey!
 The fiddle-bow went playing.

With eager haste into the mass
He hotly pressed, against a lass
 His elbow sharply sending;
The blooming wench turned quick about,
And cried, "You gawky, stupid lout!"
  Huzza! Huzza!
  Hey-day-héy! Hey! Hey!
 "Your manners need amending."

Still swiftly sped the dance-delight
From right to left, from left to right,
 The petticoats a-flying;

Until at last, all red and warm,
They rested, panting, arm in arm,
    Huzza!　Huzza!
    Hey-day-héy!　Hey!　Hey!
    With hips 'gainst elbows lying.

"Stand off, good sir! come not so near!
Full many a one his dearest dear
    Has cheated in Love's riddle!"
But ah! he wheedled her aside,
While from the Linden sounded wide
    Huzza!　Huzza!
    Hey-day-héy!　Hey!　Hey!
The shouts, and screams, and fiddle!

FAUST'S WAGER

(FROM GOETHE'S FAUST)

Faust.   Should I lie down on couch of indolence contented,

Then be it o'er with me at once!

Canst thou with guileful praise so gull me,

That self-approval swells my breast;

Canst thou with pleasure's froth delude me,

Then be that day my very last!

This wager offer I.

Mephisto.   Agreed!

Faust.   And quickly too!

If I bespeak the passing moment,

"Oh, stay, so beautiful thou art!"

Then mayst thou clap me fast in fetters,

Then utter ruin be my part!

Then let the death-bell sound its numbers,

Then be thou from thy service free,

The clock may stop, its hands be broken,

And Time be past and gone for me!

MARGARET AT THE SPINNING WHEEL.

(FROM GOETHE'S FAUST)

My heart is heavy,
My peace is o'er,
No more I'll find it,
No, nevermore.

Not him to have
Is as the grave,
And bitter all
The world as gall.

Oh, this poor head
Of mine is crazed,
And my poor sense
Is racked and dazed.

My heart is heavy,
My peace is o'er,
No more I'll find it,
No, nevermore.

From the window I
Him only would see,
When I quit the house
'Tis with him to be.

His stately step,
His figure grand,
His mouth's witching smile,
His eye of command,

His talk that flows
Like stream of bliss,
His hand's fond clasp,
And ah, his kiss!

My heart is heavy,
My peace is o'er,
No more I'll find it,
No, nevermore.

My bosom strains
Toward him fore'er;
Oh, could I fold
And hold him there!

And kiss him till
My heart ran dry,
And on his kisses
Enraptured die!

THE HUNTER OF THE ALPS

(AFTER SCHILLER)

Wilt thou, son, not guard the lambkin—
    Lambkin mild, my dearest charge;
Feeding from the grasses' flowers,
    Playing by the brooklet's marge?
Mother, mother, let me go
Up the mountain with my bow!

Wilt thou not call up the cattle
    With the lively, echoing horn?
Clearly sound the bells and sweetly,
    On the forest breezes borne.
Mother, mother, say I may
In the mountain's wildness play.

Wilt thou not attend the flowers
    Standing kindly in their bed?
Gardens there do not invite thee,
    Wild the mountain's rugged head.
Let the buds untended blow;
Mother, mother, let me go!

And the boy with bounding gladness
    Sallies forth upon the chase;
Rashly reckless, blindly venturing
    To the mountain's darkest place,
Where before the hunter fell
Flies like wind the scared gazelle.

Up the ribs of rocks all naked,
    Flies she with the nimblest step;
Over crags' wide-gaping fissures
    Speeds she with unerring leap;
But behind, the heedless boy
Follows fast with murderous joy.

Now, of all the rugged summits
    Hangs she on the highest place,
Where the cliffs sink down abruptly,
    With of path no sign or trace;

Steepy heights she sees below,
And behind, the nearing foe.

With dumb, pleading look of anguish
    Begs she mercy of her foe ;
Begs in vain, for now the arrow
    Threats to leave the bended bow ;—
When from out the rock's cleft face
Steps the Genius of the place ;

And with hand of God-like seeming
    Frees the beast as thunders he :
" Must thou death and woe be sending
    So they cry even up to me ?
Earth for each and all has room,
Why dost mark my herd for doom ? "

LOVE AND TIME

(FROM A PROSE TRANSLATION BY PROFESSOR ALBIN
PUTZKER OF A MODERN GREEK POEM)

My Dear and I one summer day
Toiled up the mountain's rugged way,
And as we slowly fared along
With heartening speech and snatch of song,
Eros and Chronos with us walked,
And lightly laughed and gayly talked.

But as we traveled, Love and Time
Began to fast and faster climb;
When cried I out, "Sweet Eros, stay,
Oh, do not, do not, haste away;
My Love can scarce maintain thy pace,
And fain would rest a little space."

But no response or word came back
Along the mountain's winding track,
But spreading out their wings, the two
Now faster and still faster flew,
Until I saw in wild dismay
Their figures fleeting fast away,

And shouted, till my breast was sore,

My earnest pleading o'er and o'er:

"My friends, Oh, whither do you fly?

Is it to place beyond my cry?

My love no farther step can go,

And will you then desert her so?"

But all in vain: their rapid flight

Soon bore them from my straining sight,

And as they vanished, on mine ear

Fell saddest words a man might hear:

"Know'st not the truth, which lives for aye,

That Love with Time will flit away?"

THE SOLDIER'S FATE

(FROM THE GERMAN OF PROFESSOR ALBIN PUTZKER)

Now tumultuous war

Draws the youth afar

Out from fatherland

Unto alien strand.

Wounded on the field of battle lies,

Underneath the blistering torrid skies,

Bleeding fast, the son, the child so dear,
His belovèd, helping ones not near.
>How the wound burns!—Oh,
>Who his pains can know!
>Anguished to the bone
>Lies he there alone.

Round him only matted jungles grow
Where the fatal ball has laid him low;
Noxious marsh is all his pillow there,
And his cover nought but stifling air.
>Now into his breast,
>Where life's joys had pressed,
>Creeps with blasting breath
>He, sole rescuer—death.

"Mother, dearest," soft he murmurs o'er;
And the burning wound then burns no more;
From his tender heart all pain has gone;
Ours in bitter grief to suffer on.

BENEDICTION

My Mother dear, these songs of many days
Are now the world's to scorn, or blame, or praise;
But could they shine with something of the grace
That bloomlike lay upon thy lovely face,
The best of them might well aspire to rise
In Love's own arms to Fame's star-gloried skies.
It may be that an idle dream I chase;
But Spirit blest, from thy exalted place
Oh, bend above them and with angel heart
Give them thy blessing as they now depart.

INDEX